"If I'm here past midnight, does that mean I have to stay for the next hundred years?" he joked.

Kayla was standing so close to him, Alain could feel the heat coming from her body. Could feel the urges being roused in his own.

All he had to do, he thought, was reach up and pull her down to his lap.

And kiss her.

Kayla took a step back. Or tried to. It felt as if she was trying to walk with a layer of glue spread across the bottom of her shoes.

And then he did it. Hands bracketing her hips, Alain drew her onto his lap.

"You shouldn't be doing this."

"It's a kiss," he whispered softly. "Just a kiss, nothing more."

Get off his lap, something inside her cried. *Now. Before it's too late.*

But it was already too late.

Dear Reader,

Well, here we are, at the end of the road, reading about the fall of the last of Lily Moreau's sons. Alain Dulac is the youngest of her offspring and just possibly the most confirmed bachelor. Tall, blond and blue-eyed, Alain can have any girl he wants and his date book is more than filled with lovely women—as deep as the pages in that book. After seeing how little luck his mother had when it came to finding a life-long partner, Alain is determined not to form any serious relationships. Why bother? But fate has something different in mind for him when a driving rainstorm has him swerving into a tree to avoid hitting a dog. The dog belongs to Kayla McKenna, one of several she is caring for. She pries Alain out of his car and takes care of his wounds—both his physical and emotional ones. And soon Alain starts to think that maybe this bachelor life really isn't for him after all.

I hope you've enjoyed this trilogy. As always, I thank you for reading and I wish you love. It makes everything else worthwhile.

Marie Ferrarella

MARIE FERRARELLA

CAPTURING THE MILLIONAIRE

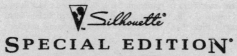

Silhouette

SPECIAL EDITION

Published by Silhouette Books

America's Publisher of Contemporary Romance

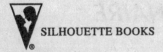

SILHOUETTE BOOKS

ISBN-13: 978-0-373-24863-6
ISBN-10:   0-373-24863-6

CAPTURING THE MILLIONAIRE

Copyright © 2007 by Marie Rydzynski-Ferrarella

Visit Silhouette Books at www.eHarlequin.com

Printed in U.S.A.

Books by Marie Ferrarella

MARIE FERRARELLA

This *USA TODAY* bestselling and RITA® Award-winning author has written more than one hundred and fifty novels for Silhouette Books, some under the name Marie Nicole. Her romances are beloved by fans worldwide.

To
Debby, Amy, Maria
And
All the other wonderful volunteers at
The German Shepherd Rescue of Orange County,
Thank you for Audrey

Chapter One

It wasn't supposed to rain in October. Not in Southern California, anyway.

Alain Dulac was pretty sure it was a law written down somewhere, like the requirements for Camelot. As he tried to steer his sports car, a vehicle definitely not meant for this kind of weather, he found that his visibility was next to zero. Because, as the old song from the sixties went, it never rained in California—but it poured.

And that's what it was doing now. Pouring. Pouring as if the entire Pacific Ocean had gotten absorbed into the black clouds that were hovering overhead and were now dumping their contents all over him. He would have been alert to the possibility of a flash flood—if he could see more than an inch or so in front of him. He wasn't even sure where he was anymore. For all he knew, he could have gotten turned around and was headed back to Santa Barbara.

By the clock, it was a little after 4:00 p.m. But to all appearances, it looked like the beginning of the Apocalypse. There was even the rumble of thunder, another unheard of event this time of year.

His windshield wipers were fighting the good fight, but it was obvious they were losing. A few seconds of visibility were all their efforts awarded him.

Alain swallowed a curse as the car hit a pocket of some sort and wobbled before continuing on its road to nowhere.

It would have been nice if the weatherman had hinted at this storm yesterday, or even early this morning, he thought darkly. He gripped the steering wheel harder, as if that could afford him better control over his car. If there had been the slightest indication that today was going to turn into something that would have made Noah shudder, Alain would have postponed going up to Santa Barbara to get that deposition until the beginning of next week.

Archie Wallace certainly looked healthy enough

to hang around until Monday. At age eighty-four, the former valet—or gentleman's gentleman, Alain believed the old term was—looked healthier than a good many men half his age. Alain could have waited to get the man's testimony instead of risking life, limb and BMW the way he was right now.

That's what he got for going into family law instead of criminal law. Not that, he'd discovered, there weren't a host of criminal activities going on behind the so-called innocent smiles of the people who came into his firm's office.

For the first time since he'd left Archie's quaint cottagelike home, a hint of a smile curved Alain's lips. Nothing wrong with camera time, he thought. As he turned the notion over in his head, he found that he liked the idea of getting his own spotlight instead of being in one by proxy. Heretofore his main claim to fame was being the youngest of Lily Moreau's sons. His mother, God bless her, was as famous for her lifestyle as she was for her exotically colorful paintings. At times her lifestyle overshadowed her work.

Alain had no doubt that the reporters who'd come to cover her last show were as interested in the dark, handsome, quarter-of-a-century-younger man at her side as they were in the latest paintings that were on display. Kyle Autumn was Alain's mother's protégé and, to hear her talk about him, the love of her life.

At least for this month.

The fact that Alain and his two older brothers each had a different father bore testimony to the fact that Lily loved her men with a passion. But that passion was anything but steadfast.

She was a better mother than she was spouse, and, luckily for the art world, a better artist than she was either of the two.

Alain had no real complaints on that score, though. Long ago he'd realized that Lily was as good a mother as she could be, and he and Georges had always had Philippe. As the oldest, Philippe was more like a father than a brother, and it was from him that Alain had gotten most of his values.

In a way, he supposed that Philippe was responsible for his having gone into family law. Philippe had always maintained that family was everything.

Too bad the Hallidays didn't feel that way. The latest case he was handling was already on its way to becoming this year's family drama. All sorts of accusations were being hurtled back and forth with wild abandon. And the tabloids were having a field day.

To be honest, it wasn't the sort of case Dunstan, Jewison and McGuire ordinarily handled. The venerable hundred-and-two-year-old firm took pride in conducting all matters with decorum and class. This case, however, had all the class of a cable reality program.

But there was an obscenely huge amount of money involved. The firm's share for winning the case for the bereaved and voluptuous widow was something only a saint would have been able to turn away from. The company had had little to keep it going but its reputation these last few years. Which was why Alain had been brought in. He was the youngest at the firm. The next in line was Morris Greenwood, and he was fifty-two. Clearly an infusion of young blood—and money—was needed.

Alain had been the one to bring the Halliday case to the older partners' attention. When they won the case—when, not if—it would also lure a great deal of business their way. Nothing wrong with that.

Like his mother, Alain was a wheeler-dealer when he had to be. He felt fairly confident that winning wouldn't present a problem. Ethan Halliday had become so smitten with his young bride that two months into the marriage, he'd had the prenup agreement torn up, and rewritten his will. The young and nubile lingerie model was to inherit more than ninety-eight percent of Halliday's considerable fortune. The will literally snatched away what the four Halliday children considered their birthright. Two men and two women, all older than their father's widow, found themselves in agreement for the first time in years, and had banded together against a common enemy: their wicked stepmother.

It had all the makings of a low-grade movie of the week. Or, in another era, a sad Grimms' fairy tale. And it looked as if the happy ending was going to be awarded to his client, if he had anything to say about it.

If he lived to deliver the deposition he'd gotten.

Another sharp skid had Alain jerking to awareness again, his mind on the immediate situation rather than the courtroom. He could all but feel the tires going out from under him.

The winds weren't helping, either. Strong gusts sporadically rose out of nowhere, fighting for possession of his vehicle. Fighting and very nearly winning. Once again he gripped the steering wheel as hard as he could just to keep the car from being shoved off the road.

It felt as if the wind had split in half, and each side was taking a turn at pushing him first in one direction, then the other, like a battered hockey puck.

Alain thought about the way the day was supposed to have gone before this sudden, spur-of-the-moment disaster had unfolded. He'd made arrangements to go antique browsing with Rachel, then grab an early, intimate dinner, after which whatever came up, came up.

Alain grinned despite the immediate trying situation. Rachel Reed was a wildcat in bed and pleasantly straightforward and uncomplicated when she was upright and dealing with life. Just the way he liked them. All fun, no seriousness, no strings. In that respect, he was very much like his mother.

He found himself struggling with the wheel again, trying to keep his car on course. Whatever that was at this point.

Where the hell was he, anyway?

Though he knew it was futile, Alain looked expectantly at the GPS system mounted on his dashboard. It continued doing what it had been doing for the last fifteen minutes: winking like a flirtatious teenager with something in her eye. One of the arrival-time readings that had flashed at him earlier had him back at his house already.

He only wished.

"What good are you if you don't work?" he demanded irritably. As if in response, the GPS system suddenly went dark. "Hey, don't be that way. I'm sorry, okay? Turn back on."

But it remained dark, as did the rest of his dashboard. He no longer had lights to guide him, and all that was coming from his high-definition radio was an endless supply of static.

Alain blew out a breath. He felt like the last man on earth, fighting the elements.

And lost, really lost.

Even his cell phone wasn't working. He'd already tried it more than once. The signal simply wasn't getting through. Mother Nature had declared war on him and all his electronic gadgets. It was as if she knew that without them, he had no sense of direction and was pretty much adrift, like a leaf in a gale.

There was a map tucked into a pocket of the front passenger door, but it was completely useless since it only encompassed Los Angeles and Orange County, and he was somewhere below Santa Barbara, on his way to Oz—or hell, whichever was closer.

He was crawling now, searching desperately for some sign of civilization. He'd left the city behind some time ago, and he knew there were homes out here somewhere because he'd passed them on his way up. But they were sparse and far apart and he'd be damned if he could see so much as a glimmer of a light coming from any building or business establishment.

He couldn't even make out the outline of any structure.

Squinting, Alain leaned forward, hunching over his steering wheel and trying to make out something—anything—in front of him.

Just as he gave up hope, he saw something dart into his path.

An animal?

His heart leaping into his throat, his instincts taking over, Alain swerved to the left in order not to hit whatever it was he'd seen. Tires squealed, brakes screamed, mud flew and he could have sworn the car took on a life of its own.

Where that tree on his left came from he had absolutely no idea. All Alain knew was that he couldn't slam into it, not if he wanted to walk away alive.

But the car that he had babied as if it were a living, breathing thing had a different plan. And right now, it wanted to become one with the tree.

A moment after it started, Alain realized that he was spinning out.

From somewhere in the back of his head, he remembered that you were supposed to steer into a spin. But everything else within him screamed that he *not* make contact with the tree if he could avoid it. So he yanked hard on the wheel, turning it as far as he could to the right.

Horrible noises assaulted his ears as the screech of the car's tires, the whine of metal and the howl of the wind became one. His usual composure melted as genuine panic gripped him. Alain heard something go pop.

And then there was nothing.

It seemed as if Winchester had been giving her problems since the day she'd found him and brought him home from the animal shelter. But she had a soft spot in her heart for the dog and cut him more than his share of slack. Of all the canines Kayla McKenna had taken in, his was one of the saddest stories.

Before she'd rescued the small German shepherd, someone had used him for target practice. When the dog had come to her attention, Winchester had a bullet in his front right leg and was running a low-grade fever because an infection had set in. Rather than go through the expense of removing the object, the local animal shelter, where she'd found the wounded dog on her bimonthly rounds, had only placed a splint on the leg.

The dog she'd whimsically named Winchester, after a rifle made popular during the winning of the West, was down to only a few hours before termination when she'd come across him. The instant she'd insisted that the attendant open up his cage, Winchester had come hobbling out and laid his head on her lap. Kayla was a goner from that moment on.

It was her habit to frequent the shelters every few weeks or so, looking for German shepherds that had, for one reason or another, been abandoned or turned out. If she could she would have taken *all* the dogs home with her, to treat, nurse and groom for adoption into good, loving homes. But even she, with her huge heart, knew she had to draw the line somewhere.

So she made her choice based on her childhood. Hailey had been her very first dog when she was a little girl—a big, lovable, atypical shepherd. As a guard dog, she was a complete failure, but she was so affectionate she'd stolen Kayla's heart from the start. Her parents had had the dog spayed, so she never had any puppies. But in a way, Kayla thought of Hailey as the mother of all the dogs she'd rescued since moving back here after getting her degree.

Kayla had all but lost count of the number of dogs she'd taken into her home, acting as foster guardian until such time as someone came along to adopt them. It didn't hurt matters that she was also a vet, so that the cost of caring for the neglected, often battered animals was nominal.

"You'll never get rich this way," Brett had sneered condescendingly. "And if you want me to marry you, you're going to have to get rid of these dogs. You know that, don't you?"

Yes, she thought now, lifting the lantern she'd brought out with her, to afford some sort of visibility in the driving rain. She'd known that, and hadn't wanted to acknowledge it. She'd met Brett in school. He was gorgeous, and she had fallen wildly in love. But it turned out she had completely misjudged him. He was *not* the man she could spend the rest of her life with.

So she'd kept the dogs and gotten rid of her fiancé and in her heart, she knew that she had made the better deal.

The wind shifted, lashing at her from the front now instead of the back. She tried to pull her hood down with her other hand, but the gusts had other ideas, ripping it from her fingers. Her hair was soaked in a matter of seconds.

"Winchester!"

The wind stole her breath before Kayla could finish calling for the German shepherd.

Damn it, dog, why did you have to run off today of all days? This wasn't the first time he'd disappeared on her. Winchester was exceedingly nervous—the result of mistreatment, no doubt— and any loud noise could send him into hiding.

"Winchester, please, come back!" The futility of her plea seemed to mock her as the wind brought her words back to her. "Taylor, we need to find him," she said to the dog on her left.

Taylor was one of the dogs she'd decided to keep for herself. He was at least seven, and no one wanted an old dog. They represented mounting bills because of health problems, and heartache because their time was short. But Kayla felt that every one of God's creatures deserved love—with the possible exception of Brett.

Suddenly, both Taylor and Ariel, the dog at her other side, began to bark.

"What? You see something?" she asked the animals.

Shading her eyes with her free hand, she raised the lantern higher with the other. As she squinted against the all but blinding rain, Kayla thought she saw what it was that Taylor and Ariel were barking at.

What all *three* of her dogs were barking at, because she could suddenly make out Winchester's shape. He was there, too, not more than five feet away from the cherry-red vehicle that, from this vantage point, seemed to be doing the impossible: it looked as if it were climbing up the oak tree. Its nose and front tires were more than a foot off the ground, urgently pressed up against the hundred-year-old trunk.

Despite the rain, Kayla could swear that she smelled the odor of smoke even from where she was standing.

One second her legs were frozen, the next she was pumping them, running toward the car as fast as she could. The rain lashed against her skin like a thousand tiny needles.

She almost slid into a rear wheel as she reached the vehicle. Rain had somehow gotten into the lantern and almost put the flame out. There was just enough light for her to see into the interior of the disabled sports car.

Dimly, Kayla could make out the back of a man's head. His face appeared to be all but swallowed up by the air bag that had deployed.

She heard a groan and realized it was coming from her, not him.

Her runaway, Winchester, was hopping on his hind legs, as if to tell her that he had discovered the man first. This had to be the canine variation on "He followed me home, can I keep him?"

The man wasn't moving.

Kayla held her breath. Was the driver just unconscious, or——?

"This is the part where I tell you to go for help," she murmured to the dogs, trying to think. "If there was someone to go get."

Which there wasn't. She lived alone and the closest neighbor was more than three miles away. Even if she could send the dogs there, no one would understand why they were barking. More than likely they'd call the sheriff, or just ignore the animals.

In either case, it did her no good. She was on her own here.

Setting the lantern down, Kayla tried the driver's door. At first it didn't budge, but she put her whole weight into pulling it. After several mighty tugs, miraculously, the door gave way. Kayla stumbled backward and would have fallen into the mud had the tree not been at her back. She slammed into it, felt the vibration up and down her spine, jarring her teeth.

She hung on to the door handle for a moment, trying to get her breath. As she drew in moist air, she stared into the car. The driver's face was still buried in the air bag, and the seat belt had a tight grip on the rest of him, holding him in place. Admitted to the party, the rain was now leaving its mark, hungrily anointing every exposed part of the stranger and soaking him to the skin.

And he still wasn't moving.

Chapter Two

"Mister. Hey, mister." Kayla raised her voice to be heard above the howl of the wind. "Can you hear me?"

When there was no response, she shook the man by the shoulder. Again, nothing happened. The stranger didn't lift his head, didn't try to move or make a sound. He was as still as death.

The uneasiness she felt began to grow. What if he was seriously injured, or—?

"Oh, God," Kayla murmured under her breath.

Moving back a foot, she nearly stepped on Winchester. The dog was hobbling about as if he had every intention of leaping into the car and reviving the stranger. At this rate, she was going to wind up stomping on one of his good legs.

"Stay out of the way, boy," Kayla ordered, and he reluctantly obeyed.

She frowned. The air bag was not deflating, but still took up all the available space on the driver's side. After having possibly saved his life, it was, in effect, smothering the man.

Kayla pushed against the bag, but it didn't give. She tried hitting it with the side of her hand, hoping to make the huge tan, marshmallow-like pillow deflate.

It didn't.

Desperate, Kayla put the lantern down on the wet ground and felt around in her pockets. In the morning, when she got dressed, she automatically put her cell phone in her pocket, along with the old Swiss army knife that had once been her father's prized possession.

A smile of relief crossed her lips as her fingers came in contact with a small, familiar shape. Quickly taking it out, she unfolded the largest blade and jabbed the air bag with it. Air whooshed out as the bag deflated.

The moment it was flat, the stranger's head fell forward, hitting the steering wheel. He was obviously still unconscious, or at least she hoped so. The alternative was gruesome.

Kayla felt the side of his neck with her finger-tips and found a pulse. "Lucky," she muttered under her breath.

The next step was to free him from the car. She'd seen accidents where the vehicle was so badly mangled, the fire department had to be summoned, with its jaws of life. Fortunately, this wasn't one of those cases. Considering the conditions, the driver had been incredibly lucky. She wondered if he'd been drinking. But a quick sniff of the air near his face told her he hadn't been.

Just another Southern Californian who didn't know how to drive in the rain, she thought. Leaning over him, she struggled to find the release button for the seat belt.

Was it her imagination, or was he stirring? God knew she hadn't been this close to a man in a very long time.

"Have…we…met?"

Sucking in her breath, Kayla jerked back, hitting her head against the car roof as she heard the hoarsely whispered question.

She swallowed. "You're awake," she declared in stunned relief.

"Or…you're…a dream," Alain mumbled weakly. Was that his voice? It sounded so high, so distant. And his eyelids, oh God, his eyelids felt heavier than a ton of coal. They kept trying to close.

Was he hallucinating? He heard barking. The hounds of hell? *Was* he in hell?

Alain tried to focus on the woman in front of him. He was delirious, he concluded. There was no other explanation for his seeing a redheaded angel in a rain slicker.

Kayla looked at the stranger closely. There was blood oozing from a wide gash on his forehead just above his right eyebrow and his eyes kept rolling upward. He looked as if he was going to pass out again at any moment. She slipped her arm around his waist, still trying to find the seat belt's release button.

"Definitely…a dream," Alain breathed as he felt her fingers feathering along his thigh. Damn, if he'd known hell was populated by creatures like this, he would have volunteered to go a long time ago.

Finding the button, she pressed it and tugged away his seat belt. Kayla looked up at his face. His eyes were shut.

"No, no, don't fade on me now," she begged. Getting the stranger to her house was going to be next to impossible if he was unconscious. She was strong, but not that strong. "Stay with me. Please," she urged.

To her relief, the stranger opened his eyes again. "Best…offer…I've had…all day," he said, wincing with every word that left his lips.

"Terrific," she murmured. "Of all the men to crash into my tree, I have to get a playboy."

Moving her fingers along his ribs gingerly, she was rewarded with another series of winces. He must have cracked or bruised them, she thought in dismay.

"Okay, hang in there," she told him as she slowly moved his torso and legs, so that he was facing out of the vehicle. With effort, she placed her arm beneath his shoulder and grasped his wrist with her hand.

The man's eyes remained closed, but he mumbled against her ear, "You shouldn't…put your trees… where…people can…hit them."

Kayla did her best to block the shiver that his breath created. Gritting her teeth against the effort she was about to make, she promised, "I'll keep that in mind." Spreading her feet, she braced herself, then attempted to rise while holding him. She felt him sagging. "Work with me here, mister."

She thought she heard a chuckle. "What…did you have…in…mind?"

"Definitely not what *you* have in mind," she assured him. Taking a deep breath, she straightened. The man she was trying to rescue was all but a dead weight.

Curling her arm around his waist as best she could, she focused on making the long journey across her lawn to her front door.

"Sorry…" His single word was carried away in the howling wind. The next moment, its meaning became clear: the man had passed out.

"No, no, wait," Kayla pleaded frantically, but it was too late.

He went down like a ton of bricks. She almost pitched forward with him, but let go at the last moment. Frustrated, she looked at the blond, striking stranger. Unconscious, he was just too much for her to carry.

She glanced back toward the house. So near and yet so far.

Catching her lower lip between her teeth, Kayla thought for a moment as all three of the dogs closed ranks around the fallen stranger. And then a rather desperate idea occurred to her. "There's more than one way to skin a cat."

Taylor barked enthusiastically, as if to add a coda to her words. Kayla couldn't help grinning at the large animal.

"You'd like that, wouldn't you? Okay, gang." She addressed the others as if they were her assistants. "Watch over him. I'll be right back."

The dogs appeared to take in every word. Kayla was a firm believer that animals understood what you said, as long as you were patient enough to train them from the time you brought them into your house. Just like babies.

"Oilcloth, oilcloth," she chanted under her breath as she hurried into her house, "what did I do with that oilcloth?" She remembered buying more then ten yards of the fabric—bright red—last year. There'd been a healthy-size chunk left over. She could swear she'd seen the remainder recently.

Crossing the kitchen, she went into the garage, still searching. The oilcloth was neatly folded and tucked away in a corner. Kayla grabbed it and quickly retraced her steps.

She was back at the wrecked vehicle and her still unconscious guest almost immediately. Spying her approach, Winchester hobbled to meet her halfway, then pivoted on his hind legs to lead her back.

"Think I forgot the way?" she asked him.

Winchester took the Fifth.

As the rain continued to lash at her, Kayla spread the oilcloth, shiny side down, on the muddy ground beside the stranger. Working as quickly as she could, rain still lashing unrelentingly at her face, she rolled the man onto the cloth. His clothes had been muddied in the process, but it couldn't be helped. Leaving him out here, bleeding and in God only knew what kind of condition, was definitely not a viable option.

"Okay," she said to her dogs, "now comes the hard part. Times like this, a sled would really come in handy." Winchester yipped, looking up at her with adoring eyes. She was, after all, his savior. "Easy for you to say," she told him.

Gripping the ends of the oilcloth, one corner in each hand, she faced the house. "Here goes nothing," she muttered under her breath, and began the long, painfully slow journey of pulling him, hoping that the stranger, with his upturned face, didn't drown on the way.

The first thing Alain became aware of as he slowly pried his eyes opened, was the weight of the anvil currently residing on his forehead. It felt as if it weighed a thousand pounds, and a gaggle of devils danced along its surface, each taking a swing with his hammer as he passed.

The second thing he became aware of was the feel of the sheets against his skin. Against almost *all* of his skin. He was naked beneath the blue-and-white down comforter. Or close to it. He definitely felt linen beneath his shoulders.

Blinking, he tried very hard to focus his eyes.

Where the hell was he?

He had absolutely no idea how he had gotten here—or what he was doing here to begin with.

Or, for that matter, who that woman with the shapely hips was.

Alain blinked again. He wasn't imagining it. There was a woman with her back to him, a woman with sumptuous hips, bending over a fireplace. The glow from the hearth, and a handful of candles scattered throughout the large, rustic-looking room provided the only light to be had.

Why? Where was the electricity? Had he crossed some time warp?

Nothing was making any sense. Alain tried to raise his head, and instantly regretted it. The pounding intensified twofold.

His hand automatically flew to his forehead and came in contact with a sea of gauze. He slowly moved his fingertips along it.

What had happened?

Curious, he raised the comforter and sheet and saw he still had on his briefs. There were more bandages, these wrapped tightly around his chest. He was beginning to feel like some sort of cartoon character.

Alain opened his mouth to get the woman's attention, but nothing came out. He cleared his throat before making another attempt, and she heard him.

She turned around—as did the pack of dogs that were gathered around her. Alain realized that she'd been putting food into their bowls.

Good, at least they weren't going to eat him.

Yet, he amended warily.

"You're awake," she said, looking pleased as she crossed over to him. The light from the fireplace caught in the swirls of red hair that framed her face. She moved fluidly, with grace. Like someone who was comfortable within her own skin. And why not? The woman was beautiful.

Again, he wondered if he was dreaming.

"And naked," he added.

A rueful smile slipped across her lips. He couldn't tell if it was light from the fire or if a pink hue had just crept up her cheeks. In any event, it was alluring.

"Sorry about that."

"Why, did you have your way with me?" he asked, a hint of amusement winning out over his confusion.

"You're not naked," she pointed out. "And I prefer my men to be conscious." Then she became serious. "Your clothes were all muddy and wet. I managed to wash them before the power went out completely." She gestured about the room, toward the many candles set on half the flat surfaces. "They're hanging in my garage right now, but they're not going to be dry until morning," she said apologetically. "If then."

He was familiar with power outages; they usually lasted only a few minutes. "Unless the power comes back on."

The redhead shook her head, her hair moving about her face like an airy cloud. "Highly doubtful. When we lose power around here, it's hardly ever a short-term thing. If we're lucky, we'll get power back by midafternoon tomorrow."

Alain glanced down at the coverlet spread over his body. Even that slight movement hurt his neck. "Well, as intriguing as the whole idea might be, I really can't stay naked all that time. Can I borrow some clothes from your husband until mine are ready?"

Was that amusement in her eyes, or something else? "That might not be so easy," she told him.

"Why?"

"Because I don't have one."

He'd thought he'd seen someone in a hooded rain slicker earlier. "Significant other?" he suggested. When she made no response, he continued, "Brother? Father?"

She shook her head at each suggestion. "None of the above."

"You're alone?" he questioned incredulously.

"I currently have seven dogs," she told him, amusement playing along her lips. "Never, at any time of the night or day, am I alone."

He didn't understand. If there was no other person in the house—

"Then how did you get me in here? You sure as hell don't look strong enough to have carried me all the way by yourself."

She pointed toward the oilcloth she'd left spread out and drying before the fireplace. "I put you in that and dragged you in."

He had to admit he was impressed. None of the women he'd ever met would have even attempted to do anything like that. They would likely have left him out in the rain until he was capable of moving on his own power. Or drowned.

"Resourceful."

"I like to think so." And, being resourceful, her mind was never still. It now attacked the problem of the all-but-naked man in her living room. "You know, I think there might be a pair of my dad's old coveralls in the attic." As she talked, Kayla started to make her way toward the stairs, and then stopped. A skeptical expression entered her bright-green eyes as they swept over the man on the sofa.

Alain saw the look and couldn't help wondering what she was thinking. Why was there a doubtful frown on her face? "What?"

"Well…" Kayla hesitated, searching for a delicate way to phrase this, even though her father had been gone for some five years now. "My dad was a pretty big man."

Alain still didn't see what the problem was. "I'm six-two."

She smiled, and despite the situation, he found himself being drawn in as surely as if someone had thrown a rope over him and begun to pull him closer.

"No, not big—" Kayla held her hand up to indicate height "—big." This time, she moved her hand in front of her, about chest level, to denote a man whose build had been once compared to that of an overgrown grizzly bear.

"I'll take my chances," Alain assured her. "It's either that or wear something of yours, and I don't think either one of us wants to go that route."

It suddenly occurred to him that he was having a conversation with a woman whose name he didn't know and who didn't know his. While that was not an entirely unusual situation for him, an introduction was definitely due.

"By the way, I'm Alain Dulac."

Her smile, he thought, seemed to light up the room far better than the candles did.

"Kayla," she told him. "Kayla McKenna." She saw him wince as he tried to sit up to shake her hand. Rather than a handshake, she gently pressed her palms against his shoulders and pushed him back down on the sofa. "I think you should stay there for a while. You gashed your head and cracked a couple of ribs. I sewed your forehead and taped you up," she added. "Nothing else appears to be damaged. I ran my portable scanner over you."

Other than running into someone from *Star Trek,* there was only one conclusion to be drawn. "I take it you're a doctor?"

Kayla shook her head. "Vet," she corrected.

"Oh." Gingerly, Alain touched the bandage around his head again, as if he wasn't quite sure what to expect. "Does that mean I'm suddenly going to start barking, or have an overwhelming urge to drink out of the toilet anytime soon?"

She laughed, and he caught himself thinking that it was a very sexy sound.

"Only if you want to. The basics of medicine, whether for an animal or a human being, are surprisingly similar," she assured him. "They don't even automatically shoot horses anymore when they break their legs these days." He began to stir, then stopped when she looked at him a tad sternly. "Why don't you rest while I go see if I can find my dad's clothes in the attic?"

Without his realizing it, the pack of dogs in the room had closed in on him. They appeared to be eyeing him suspiciously. At least, that was the way it seemed to him. There were seven in all, seven German shepherds of varying heights and coloration: two white, one black and the rest black-and-tan. And none of them, except for the little guy with the cast, looked to be overly friendly.

Alain raised his eyes toward Kayla. "Are you sure it's safe to leave me with these dogs?"

She smiled and nodded. "You won't hurt them. I trust you."

"No offense, but I wasn't thinking of me hurting them. I was worried about them deciding they haven't had enough to eat tonight." He was only half kidding. "Survival of the fittest and all that."

"Don't worry." She patted his shoulder, and realized it was the same gesture she used with the dogs to reassure them. "They haven't mistaken you for an invading alpha male." She looked around at them and realized, to an outsider, they might seem a bit intimidating. "If it makes you feel any better, I'll take some of them with me."

That was a start, he allowed. "How about all of them?"

"You don't like dogs." It wasn't a question, it was a statement. She felt a bit disappointed in the man, although she wasn't entirely certain why.

"I like dogs fine," he countered. "But I prefer to be standing in their company, not lying down like the last item on their menu."

She supposed, given his present condition, she could understand his frame of mind. "Okay, they'll come with me. I'll just leave you Winchester." She nodded toward the smallest dog.

The shepherd looked friendly enough. But Alain was curious as to her reasoning. "Why? Because he broke his leg?"

"He didn't break his leg," she corrected. "Someone shot him. But I thought the two of you might form some sort of bond, because Winchester was the one who found you." She left the room with the menagerie following her, closer than a shadow.

It came to him about a minute after Kayla walked

out of the room with her four-legged entourage that she was wrong. Winchester hadn't found him; the dog had been responsible for his sudden and unexpected merging with the oak tree.

But it was too late to point that out.

Chapter Three

The door to the attic creaked as she opened it. For a moment, Kayla just stood in the doorway, looking at the shadows her lantern created within the room.

Ariel bumped her head against her thigh, as if to nudge her in.

Taking a deep breath, Kayla raised the lantern higher to illuminate the space, and walked in.

She hadn't been up here in a very long time. Not because the gathering place for spiders, crickets and all manner of other bugs held any special terror for her. She had no problem with any of God's creatures, no matter how creepy-crawly the rest of the world might find them. No, what kept her from coming up here was the bittersweet pain of memories.

The attic was filled with furniture, boxes of clothing, knickknacks and assorted personal treasures belonging to people long gone. Yet she couldn't make herself throw them out or even donate them to charity. To do so, to sweep the place clean and get rid of all the clutter, felt to her like nothing short of a violation of trust. But as much as she couldn't bring herself to part with her parents' and grandparents' possessions, coming up here, remembering people who were no longer part of her everyday life, was still extremely difficult.

Kayla treasured the paths they had walked through her life, and at the same time hated being reminded that they were gone. That the people who had made her childhood and teen years so rich were no longer there to share in her life now.

Maybe if they had been around, she wouldn't have had that low period in San Francisco....

As if sensing her feelings, the six dogs that had come racing up here now stood quietly in the shadows, waiting for her to do whatever it was she had to do.

Kayla took another long, deep breath, trying not to notice how the dust tickled her nose.

An ancient, dust-laden, black Singer sewing machine that had belonged to her great-grandmother stood like a grande dame in the corner, regally presiding over all the other possessions that had found their way up here. Her grandfather's fishing rod and lures stood in a corner, near her father's golf clubs, still brand-new beneath the covers her mother had knit for them.

Next to the clubs was a body-building machine that had belonged not to her father but her mother. Kayla's mom had been so proud of maintaining her all-but-perfect body. She'd used the machine faithfully, never missing a day. Kayla pressed her lips together to keep back the tears that suddenly filled her eyes. The cancer hadn't cared what her mother looked like on the outside, it had ravaged her within, leaving Kayla motherless by the time she was sixteen.

By twenty-two, she'd become a veritable orphan.

Now the dogs were her family.

You're getting maudlin. Snap out of it, Kayla upbraided herself.

Taking another deep breath, she blew it out slowly and then approached a large, battered steamer trunk in the corner opposite the sewing machine. The trunk had its own history. Her grandfather had come from Ireland with all his worldly possessions in that trunk. When he landed in New York, he'd discovered that someone had jimmied it open and taken everything inside. Seamus McKenna had kept the trunk, vowing to one day fill it with the finest silks and satins.

These days, her parents' things resided inside the battered container, mingling just the way they had when they'd had been alive. The contents were worth far more to Kayla than the silks and satins her grandfather had dreamed of.

The attic fairly shouted of memories. Kayla could have sworn she could see her parents standing just beyond the lantern's light.

She felt her heart ache.

"I miss you guys," she said quietly, blinking several times as she felt moisture gathering along her lashes.

All of them, especially her father, had been her inspiration. She couldn't remember a time when she hadn't wanted to be just like him, hadn't planned on going into medicine because he had. He was the kindest, gentlest man ever created....

But her passionate love for animals took her in a slightly different direction, and instead of a doctor, she'd become a veterinarian. She never once regretted her decision. Being a vet, along with the volunteer work she was presently doing for the German Shepherd Rescue Organization, had given her a sense of purpose she badly needed.

And there was another, added bonus. She didn't feel alone anymore, not with all these four-footed companions eager to display their gratitude to her at the drop of a dog treat.

Crossing to the trunk, Kayla started to open it, then stopped and glanced back at the dogs.

German shepherds, despite their tough public image as police dogs, had very delicate skins and often had a multitude of allergies. The ones she had taken into her home and was presently caring for certainly did. Three of them were on daily allergy medication.

"Maybe I should have left you downstairs," she said, thinking out loud. Well, it was too late now. "Okay, stay."

She said the last word as a command. She knew that training animals was a constant, ongoing thing, and she never missed an opportunity to reinforce any headway made. The dogs instantly turned into breathing statues. Kayla smiled to herself as she flipped the lock on the trunk and lifted the lid.

A very faint hint of the perfume her mother always wore floated up to her.

Or maybe that was just her imagination, creating the scent.

Kayla didn't care. It was real to her, and that was all that mattered. A vivid image of her mother laughing flashed through her mind's eye. Her mom had remained healthy-looking until almost the very end.

Leaving the lantern beside the trunk, Kayla carefully went through the clothes and memorabilia inside. Some of her father's old medical school textbooks lined the bottom of the trunk—he'd never liked throwing anything away. Finally, she found the overalls. They were tucked into a corner near the pile of books.

Daniel McKenna had never favored suits or ties. He tended to like wearing comfortable clothes beneath his white lab coat. Ironically, the week before he'd suddenly died, he'd told her that when he was gone, she should give away his clothes to the local charity—just as he'd always given away his time and services so generously in his off-hours.

But Kayla couldn't force herself to give away every article of clothing. For sentimental reasons, she had kept one of his outfits—his old coveralls.

Taking them out now, she held up the faded denim and shook her head. The man on her sofa was going to be lost in them. But it would do in a pinch. And, after all, it was only temporary. Just until his own clothes were dry again.

She had to admit, Kayla thought as she folded the large garment, that if she had her druthers, she would vote to have Alain Dulac remain just the way he was right now. There was no denying that beneath that blanket, he was one magnificent specimen of manhood.

Her mother would have approved of the sculpted definition in his arms, and the washboard abs. Most likely, Kayla thought with a smile, her mom would have wound up comparing workout routines with him, and giving Alain advice on how to get twice the results out of his efforts.

Not that there was really any room for improvement, she mused, her mouth curving.

Closing the lid of the trunk, Kayla stooped down and picked up the lantern again.

She hadn't seen a wedding ring on the man's hand, but that didn't really mean anything. A lot of married men didn't wear rings—and those that did could easily take them off. Although, now that she thought of it, there hadn't been a tan line on Alain's finger to indicate he played those kinds of games.

Still, she couldn't help absently wondering if there was someone waiting for Alain Dulac back home, wherever home was.

The next moment she laughed at herself. What was she thinking? Of course there was someone waiting for him. Men who looked like Alain Dulac *always* had someone waiting for them. They didn't go around creating bodies like that just because they had nothing better to do. That kind of body was bait, pure and simple. Had he reeled in his catch?

Probably more than his share.

Makes no difference one way or another, she insisted silently, leaving the attic.

She waited until her entourage had gathered around her out in the hall, then closed the door.

"Okay, gang," she announced cheerfully, "We got what we came for. Let's go."

Winchester had remained at his side, staring at him, the entire time Kayla was gone. He'd tried to pet the dog, but the very movement had sent pains shooting up and down his side.

Alain strained now, trying to hear if the woman he was indebted to was coming back. Boards squeaked overhead. She was leaving the attic, he guessed, relieved.

"Your mistress is coming," he told the dog. "You can go stare at her now."

Alain heard the sound of thirteen pairs of feet hitting the stairs, hers muffled by the clatter of the dogs'.

Damn, he wanted to sit up to greet her like a normal person, but even shifting slightly on the sofa brought the anvil devils back, swinging their hammers in double-time. Not only that, but there was an excruciating pain shooting up from his ribs.

He'd never been one to make a fuss, and he'd always thought he had a high pain threshold. When he fell out of a tree and broke his arm at the age of eight, he'd been so stoic Philippe had been certain he'd gone into shock. But this was bad. Really bad. He couldn't take in a deep breath, only shallow, small ones—which somehow fed the claustrophobia he felt. He kept trying to inhale a deep breath to hold the sensation at bay, but each failure only drew it closer.

"Why can't I take a deep breath?" he wanted to know the second Kayla walked into the living room. He was vaguely aware how the light from the lantern preceded her like a heavenly beam, illuminating her every movement. Directly behind her, her animals came pouring in.

"Because you cracked two ribs and I've taped you up tighter than a CIA secret," she answered matter-of-factly. Patient feedback—and complaints— were two things she didn't get as a vet. Being a veterinarian did have its perks, she thought. "It's only temporary."

Placing the lantern on the coffee table, she held up the coveralls.

It took him a second to realize that she wasn't unfurling a bolt of material, but an article of clothing. The man who had sired this petite woman had been huge. It was obvious that she must have taken after her mother.

"Wow, you really weren't kidding about your father being big, were you?" The coveralls looked as if they could accommodate two of him. "How much did your dad weigh?"

"Too much," she answered shortly. "Given his profession, he should have known better."

Trying to ignore the throbbing shaft of pain that kept skewering him, he tried to focus on the conversation. "What was his profession?"

"My father was a doctor. A general practitioner," she explained.

"Could have been worse," Alain allowed. When she looked at him quizzically, he said, "Your father could have been a nutritionist or a diet doctor." Forcing a resigned smile to his lips, he reached out for the coveralls she was holding, then suddenly dropped his hand as he sucked in what little breath he had to spare.

Concerned, Kayla set the coveralls on the coffee table. "Maybe you should just lie back. You can always get dressed later. God knows you're not going anywhere tonight."

As if to underline her assessment, the wind chose that moment to pick up again, rattling the windows like a prisoner trying to break out—or, in this case, in.

Kayla lightly placed her hand on Alain's forehead and then frowned.

He didn't like her reaction, Alain thought. "What's wrong?"

She drew her hand back, looking at him thoughtfully. "You feel warm."

He didn't like the way she said that, either. He really didn't have time for this. His schedule was full and he should have been on his way home. "Isn't that a good sign? Doesn't cold usually mean dead?"

"*Stiff* means dead," she corrected, with just a hint of amusement reaching her lips. "Wait here, I'm going to get you something to make you feel better."

"Wait here," he echoed when she'd gone. Winchester looked at him with what appeared to Alain's slightly fevered brain to be sympathy. "As if I had a choice."

The shepherd barked in response, apparently agreeing that, at the moment, he didn't.

Alain stared at the animal. He had to be hallucinating. What other explanation was there for his having a conversation, albeit mostly one-sided, with a dog in a cast?

This time Kayla returned more quickly. When she came back, she was holding a glass of water in one hand and an oval blue pill in the other.

"Here, take this," she instructed in a voice that left no chance for argument. She held the blue pill to his lips.

Alain raised his eyes warily. For the most part, he was as laid-back as they came. But he also wasn't a trusting fool. "What is it?"

"Just take it," she told him. "It'll make you feel better, I promise." When he still made no move to swallow the pill, she sighed. "It's a painkiller," she told him, a note of exasperation in her voice. "Do you always question everything?"

"Pretty much." Well, if she'd wanted to get rid of him, she could have done it while he was unconscious, he reasoned. So, with some reluctance, he took the pill from her, preferring to put it in his own mouth. "It's in the blood."

"What?" She raised one eyebrow quizzically. "Being annoying?"

"Being a lawyer." He placed the pill into his mouth.

Kayla shrugged at the reply. "Same thing," she quipped. Placing her hand behind his head, she raised it slightly so that he could drink the water she'd brought. As she did so, she could feel him tensing. He was obviously struggling not to show her that he was in pain. "This will help," she promised again.

He had nothing against painkillers, but the pain actually wasn't his main problem. "What'll help is if I can get back on the road," he told her. "I'm supposed to be in L.A. tonight." Rachel wasn't going to take it kindly if he rescheduled their date, and he was having too good a time with her to put a stop to it just yet.

And there was that impromptu get-together that the firm was holding. Dunstan had said there was no pressure to attend, but everyone knew there was.

The vibrant redhead was shaking her head in response to his statement. "Sorry, not going to happen. Your car is immobilized." She tucked the coverlet closer around him. "And so are you."

"My car." Flashes of the accident came back to him. Had he really driven the car up a tree, or was that some kind of nightmare? He tried to sit up, and felt not so much pain as an odd sort of murkiness pouring through his limbs. And the cloudiness was descending over his brain again. What the hell was going on? "How bad is it?"

Kayla pretended to consider the question. "That depends."

The town probably came equipped with a crooked mechanic who made his money preying on people who were passing through and had the misfortune of breaking down here, Alain thought. Everyone knew someone who had a horror story about being taken because there was no other alternative.

"On what?" he asked warily.

That, she assumed, was his lawyer look. But she could already see it fading away as the painkiller kicked in. "On whether you want a functioning vehicle or a very large paperweight."

He'd only had the car for a year. It was barely broken in. He should have gone with his first instincts and rented a vehicle to drive up to Santa Barbara. "It's totaled?"

This time she did consider his question. She really hadn't paid that much attention to the condition of his car; she'd been more concerned with getting him out of the vehicle and out of the rain.

"Maybe not totaled," she allowed, "but it's certainly not going anywhere anytime soon."

Suddenly the room seemed to be getting darker. Was the fire going out?

Or was he?

His ribs didn't hurt anymore. Maybe he could pay her for the use of her own car, he thought. His head began to do strange things. Alain tried to focus. "I can't stay here."

"Why not?" she asked innocently. "It doesn't look as if you have much choice." And then she added with a smile, "Don't worry, I'm not going to charge you rent."

Thinking was rapidly becoming difficult for him. He needed to stay on point. "I've got places to go, people to see."

"The places'll still be there tomorrow. And the day after that," she added for good measure. "And if the people are worth anything, so will they."

Kayla had no doubt that the pill was taking effect. She should have given it to him in the first place, she thought, but she'd needed his input to see how bad he was. He was going to be asleep in a few more minutes, she judged.

She sat down on the coffee table facing him. Taylor lowered his haunches and sat down beside her like a silent consort.

"Right now," she continued in a soft, soothing

voice, "you need to rest. The roads are probably flooded, so you wouldn't be going anywhere, anyway. Every time it rains like this, Shelby becomes an island."

"Shelby?" he asked groggily.

"The town you're passing through." It was hardly a dot on the map. Most people didn't even know they'd been through it. Leaning forward, Kayla placed her hand on his arm to make him feel secure. "I gave you something to make you sleep, Alain. Stop fighting it and just let it do its thing."

He liked the way his name sounded on her lips.

The thought floated through his head without preamble. He was drifting, he realized. And his limbs were growing heavier, as if they didn't belong to him anymore.

"If...I...fall asleep..." He was really struggling to get the words out now.

She leaned in closer to hear him. "Yes?"

"Will...you...have your way with me now?"

She laughed and shook her head. This one was something else.

"No," she assured him, not quite able to erase the smile from her lips. "I won't have my way with you."

"Too...bad."

And then there was no more conversation. His eyelids had won the battle and closed down.

Chapter Four

He was being watched.

The unshakable sensation of having a pair of eyes fixed on him, on his every move—from close range—bore through the oppressive, thick haze that was swirling around him.

Alain struggled to surface, to reach full consciousness and open his eyes. When he finally succeeded, only extreme control kept him from crying out in surprise.

Approximately five inches separated his face from the dog's muzzle.

Alain jerked up, drawing his elbows in under him.

The salvo of pain that shot through him registered an instant later. This time, a moan did escape.

In response, the dog reared up and licked him. Alain grimaced and made a noise that expressed something less than pleasure over the encounter.

"Welcome back."

The cheerful voice was coming from behind him. Before he could turn his head to look at her, Kayla moved into his line of vision.

She'd changed her clothes, he noticed. It looked as if she was wearing the same curve-hugging jeans, but instead of a T-shirt, she had on a green pullover sweater that played up the color of her eyes—among other things.

It took him a second to raise his gaze to her face. "How long was I out?"

She bent to pat Winchester on the head. The dog had spent the entire night at Alain's side. There was a definite attachment forming, at least from the dog's point of view.

"You slept through the night," Kayla told him. She had spent it in the chair opposite him, watching to make sure he was all right. "Rather peacefully, I might add." And then, because he'd mentioned a woman's name during the night, she couldn't resist asking, "Who's Lily?"

That question had come at him from left field. Did this woman know his mother? It seemed unlikely, given that she was wrapped up with her animals, and the only animals her mother liked were the two-legged kind. *In bed*.

Alain watched Kayla's face as he answered, "My mother. Why?"

"You called out to her once during the night." She cocked her head, curious. "You call your mother by her first name?" She'd been around six years old before she even knew her parents had other names besides Mommy and Daddy. She couldn't imagine referring to either of them by their given names.

"No, not really." Since he couldn't remember if he'd even dreamed, he hadn't a clue as to why he'd call out his mother's name, and he didn't know any other Lily. But he was more curious about something else. "You stayed up all night watching me sleep?" Why would she do that? he wondered, feeling oddly comforted by the act.

Kayla laughed as she shook her head. "We're a little rural here, but I'm not that desperate for entertainment. No, I didn't stay up all night watching you sleep. I spent part of it sleeping myself," she assured him.

In actuality, she'd spent very little of it asleep. His breathing had been labored at one point, and she'd worried that she might have given him too much of the medication, so she'd remained awake to monitor him. But she didn't feel there was any reason for Alain to know that.

"Nothing I wouldn't have done for any of my other patients," she continued nonchalantly. "Even if you don't have fur." And then she looked a little more serious. "How's the head?"

Until she asked, Alain hadn't realized that the anvil chorus was no longer practicing their latest performance inside his skull. He touched his forehead slowly as if to assure himself that it was still there.

"Headache's gone," he said in amazement. The way it had hurt last night, he'd been fairly certain it was going to split his head open. And now it was gone, as if it had never existed. Except for the state of his ribs, he actually felt pretty good.

Pleased, Kayla nodded. "Good." Moving away from the coffee table, she turned toward the kitchen. "Hungry?"

He was about to say no. He was never hungry first thing in the morning, requiring only pitch-black coffee until several hours after he was awake and at work. But this morning there was this unfamiliar pinch in his stomach. It probably had something to do with the fact that he hadn't had any dinner last night, he reasoned.

He nodded slowly in response to her question. "Yes, I am."

Kayla caught the inflection in his voice. "You sound surprised."

"I am," he admitted. "I'm not usually hungry first thing in the morning."

He was probably always too busy to notice, she guessed. People in the city tended to spin their wheels a lot, going nowhere and making good time at it. She should know; she'd been one of those people for a while. "Country air will do that to you."

Her comment surprised him. "So you consider this the country?"

That seemed like an odd thing for him to ask. "Don't you?"

Alain laughed shortly. "Last night, I considered it Oz," he admitted. "But usually 'country' means farmland to me."

She supposed there was an argument for that. To her, any place that didn't pack in a hundred people to the square yard was the country.

"There used to be nothing but farms around here. We've still got a few." And she loved to drive by them whenever she had the chance. Not to mention that the families on that acreage were always opened to taking in some of her dogs. "Corn and strawberries, mostly," she added.

Ariel was shifting from foot to foot behind her, silently reminding her that she had yet to be fed. Which brought Kayla full circle. "So, what's your pleasure?"

The question caught him up short. Without fully

realizing it, he'd been watching the way Kayla's breasts rose and fell beneath the green sweater with every breath she took.

As for her question, he wasn't about to give her the first response that came to his lips, because he doubted that the beautiful vet would see it as anything more than a come-on. And maybe it was, but he'd never meant anything more in his life. His pleasure, at the moment, involved some very intimate images of Kayla—sans the green sweater—and himself.

"Whatever you're having," he told her, glancing toward Winchester. The dog was still eyeing him, an unrelenting polygraph machine waiting for a slipup.

His answer satisfied Kayla. "Eggs and toast it is." She nodded.

The choice surprised him. Somehow, he'd just assumed that Kayla would be a vegetarian. Half the women he knew turned their noses up at anything that hadn't been plucked out of the ground, pulled down from a tree or gotten off a stalk. In addition, he would have thought that the cheerful vet would have been health conscious.

He watched her face as he said, "Don't you know eggs are bad for you?"

She shook her head. "They've been much maligned," Kayla countered. "The FDA says having four eggs a week is perfectly acceptable. Besides, an egg has a lot of nutrients to offer. My great-grand-father ate eggs every day of his life and he lived to be ninety-six."

"Might have lived to be ten years older if he'd avoided eggs," Alain deadpanned.

His quip was met with a wide grin. Something inside of him responded, lighting up, as well. "You have a sense of humor. Nice," she said.

The last word seemed to whisper along his skin, making him warmer. Since the response was some-thing a teenager might experience, Alain hadn't a clue as to what was going on with him. Maybe it was a reaction to whatever she'd given him last night.

The way he was looking at her, looking right into her, stirred up a whole host of things inside of Kayla. His smile alone made lightning flash in her veins. She didn't bother squelching it, because for once, en-tertaining these kinds of feelings was all right. She wouldn't act on it, and at the moment, she was willing to bet that he couldn't. By the time he could, he would be gone.

She held off going to the kitchen to make break-fast a moment longer. "I almost forgot. I've got some good news."

He immediately thought of the disabled BMW. "My car's all right, after all?"

His car. She hadn't even looked at it since she'd pulled him free of the wreckage. It was still raining and the power was still out, which meant the phones weren't working. There was no way to call Mick's gas station to get someone out to look at the fancy scrap of metal.

"No, your car's still embracing my tree," she told him, "but your clothes are dry, so you don't have to put on my father's coveralls." Her mouth curved into what her mother had once called her wicked grin as she added, "Unless you want to."

"If I'm going to get lost inside of someone else's clothes, I'd rather the clothes belonged to someone of the female persuasion." Preferably with her still in it, he added silently. "No offense."

"None taken," she assured him.

Was it her, or was it getting warmer in here? Kayla wondered. The fire certainly hadn't gotten more intense since she'd lit it earlier this morning.

Kayla placed the clothes that she had just gotten off the line in her garage on the coffee table in front of him. "You can put them on after breakfast, if you're up to it. How *are* you feeling?" she asked, suddenly realizing that she'd only asked about his headache, nothing more.

Alain quickly took stock of his parts before answering. His ribs were still aching, but not as badly as they had last night. And while there was no headache, he was acutely aware of the gash she must have sewn up on his forehead. It pulsed.

"Good enough for me to put my clothes on now," he told her.

She opened her mouth to say that maybe he should wait until after he ate before he went jumping into his clothes, but then she shut it again. The man should know what he was capable of doing. She wasn't his mother or his keeper.

"Okay." But being distant and removed just wasn't her way. Kayla came closer to the sofa again. "Why don't I help you to the bathroom so you can change in private?" she suggested.

He thought that was a little like closing the barn door after the horse had run off, seeing as how she'd been the one to undress him in the first place. But he didn't raise the point, since it might sound like a protest. He didn't have anything against beautiful woman doing whatever they wanted with his clothes and his body. What he didn't like was the idea of being an invalid and needing help.

"I can make it on my own," he informed her.

If he meant to make her back off, he was in for a surprise, she thought. "How do you know?" Kayla challenged. "You haven't been on your feet since I brought you in."

Instead of answering, he sat up and swung his legs out from under the bedclothes. He meant to stand up and show her that he was all right. Planting his feet on the floor, he pushed himself up off the sofa—and immediately felt the room spin.

Alain blinked his eyes as if that would help him clear his head. He was feeling as weak as a kitten with a cold. Exasperated, he stole a look in Kayla's direction.

"What the hell did you give me last night?" he demanded.

He wouldn't be familiar with the generic name of the drug she'd used, Kayla thought. There was no point in mentioning it. She kept it simple. "Just something to make you sleep."

"For how many days?" He'd lost all track of time. "Twenty?"

"Do you always exaggerate?" she replied, then answered her own question. "Oh, wait, I forgot, you're a lawyer."

This time, he thought he saw her top lip curl in a sneer. Was that her reaction to what he did for a living? Most women melted when they found out that he worked for a famous firm, equating it to wealth. "You don't place much stock in lawyers, do you?"

The land the house was on used to be twice the size it was now. A boundary dispute had brought her family into court, and the judge had ruled against them. Her grandfather had come precariously close to losing everything he'd worked for his entire adult life. Watching his spirit being bent and then all but broken had been a horrible experience for Kayla. She thought of lawyers as only slightly higher on the food chain than scorpions.

The best ones had silver tongues, but the bottom line was the same: they were all vultures. "They live off the sweat of others."

Alain nodded. "I'll take that as a no."

She was surprised that he just let the matter drop like that. "Aren't you going to try to defend your brethren? To tell me all the good that lawyers have accomplished? How the world's a better place because of attorneys?"

Alain shook his head. "I never try to pry open a closed mind. Good way to lose my fingers." And then he grinned, creating a mini-whirlpool in her stomach. "Not to mention other, equally as precious body parts."

He didn't argue what he knew he couldn't win. Intelligent as well as good-looking, she decided. "Well, I'll give you this—you're smarter than the average lawyer." As she had last night, Kayla braced herself. And then she looked down at him. "Ready?"

"For what?" Certainly not her, he added silently. There was definitely more to this woman than met the eye.

Kayla nodded to her left. "The bathroom."

There seemed to be no point in arguing with her

about his ability to get around. Alain dug his knuckles into the sofa on either side of his thighs and pushed himself up and off the cushion once more. Triumph was fleeting. As he straightened, he felt wobbly—again.

So much so that he swayed even though he was trying hard not to. Preoccupied with not falling flat on his face and on his dignity, he didn't even notice that he was still wearing only the very small black briefs he'd intended strictly for Rachel's perusal.

The next moment, he felt Kayla slip her arm through his. "Shall we?" she asked brightly.

Her eyes were looking directly into his. But from the smile he saw in them, he knew that she'd allowed herself at least one long, assessing scan of his torso. He couldn't help but wonder how he'd measured up with whoever she'd taken to her bed in earnest.

He began to walk, using what felt like someone else's legs. A disembodied feeling hovered over him with each step he took.

"The last time someone walked me into their bathroom, we wound up showering together."

"I don't recommend a shower right away," she told him. "But if you want to take one later, let me know. I'll need to get some plastic wrap for you."

A vision of the two of them, naked but wrapped together tightly in plastic, materialized in his mind. "Sounds kinky."

"For your bandages," she told him, without missing a beat. God, but he was well-built, she thought again. It was like propping up a rock wall. "You can't get them wet."

He looked down at the white gauze around his chest. "How long are they going to have to stay on?"

That depended on his healing process. "Longer than a day."

He was still taking what felt like baby steps. His knees were shaky but he wasn't altogether sure if that was due to the accident he'd had or the proximity of his escort.

Alain decided it might be a combination of both. Like his brother Georges, he could never resist a good-looking woman, and the one next to him was leagues beyond merely good-looking. However, unlike Georges, he was completely confident that settling down was not in the cards for him. When it came to that, he was too much like their mother.

Once upon a time, he'd thought that Georges was, too, but that was before he'd had met what Philippe referred to as their brother's "once in a lifetime woman." Vienna was a gentle, heart-stoppingly beautiful woman who had, without trying, changed all the dynamics in Georges's life and made him long for what he'd never had before: a steadfast relationship.

Well, for Georges's sake, Alain hoped that existed. As for himself, he knew it would never happen.

Kayla stopped walking and he realized that they must have reached the bathroom. Leaning him against the wall by the door, she slipped her arm from his and took a step back. Alain would have been amused if he wasn't perspiring so much.

"Holler if you need me," she instructed. It wasn't just a throwaway line; she meant it.

Alain remained leaning against the wall. He had his suspicions that she noticed.

"I won't need you," he assured her. "Despite what you might think of lawyers, I am capable of dressing myself. I have been doing it since I was three."

She smiled, inclining her head. If she took note of the line of perspiration along his brow, she gave no indication. "I'm sure you have."

She backed away, and that was when he realized that they hadn't reached this part of the house alone. The dogs were all in the background. But Winchester, easily the runt in this eclectic litter, was right there, front and center.

The odd thing was, the dog appeared to be looking up at *him* rather than her.

"If you need an escort back," she continued, "just send Winchester to get me. I'll be in the living room, making breakfast."

"The living room?" he echoed. "Don't you usually make it in the kitchen?"

"I do," she allowed. "When the electricity is

working. But it's not and there's a fireplace in the living room."

"You're using the fireplace?" he asked incredulously. Most of the women he knew could barely turn on a stove. Roughing it meant eating at a less than five-star restaurant.

She winked just before she turned on her heel. "Think of it as camping in."

He watched her walk away. Watched and appreciated the gentle sway of her hips with each step.

Alain roused himself with effort.

It felt like an incredibly domestic scene, he thought as he entered the bathroom. He closed the door just in time, before Winchester managed to slip in with him.

Too domestic, he decided.

He never remained for breakfast when he slept with a woman. That had less to do with his rarely having breakfast than it did with the fact that he never spent the night, no matter how long the lovemaking lasted or what hour it was finally over. Literally sleeping with someone would have opened up an entire floodgate of assumptions that had no place in his life.

The only relationships he wanted to form with the opposite sex were temporary, cursory ones. Like his mother. Lily Moreau might have been married to all three of the men who'd fathered her sons, but even those unions had dissolved for one reason or another. The other liaisons—and there had been too many to count—had all been short-lived. His mother operated by one small rule of thumb: she enjoyed her relationships, until she didn't. And then she moved on. Before they did.

Life was too short to stay in one place and wait for the inevitable pain to come.

Alain looked in the mirror. A faint, pale stubble was growing on his cheeks and chin, but otherwise, he didn't look the worse for his experience.

A noise outside the door caught his attention. He'd better get dressed before she came in to check up on him. Alain shook his head. He wasn't too sure what to make of Kayla McKenna. She was a great deal friendlier than he thought was actually prudent, given her living situation. And he couldn't help wondering why she was unattached. There had to be a story there.

Damn, just pulling on his trousers exhausted him. That accident had taken more out of him than he'd thought. Even so, he struggled to put on his socks and his shirt. For the time being, Alain left the suit jacket off.

After pausing to throw water into his face, he opened the door.

And nearly stepped on the dog with the cast.

Chapter Five

Moving back to avoid stepping on Winchester's foot, Alain grasped the door to keep from falling down himself. He swallowed a string of choice words he knew Kayla wouldn't exactly appreciate hearing.

Winchester looked up at him with adoring, liquid-brown eyes. Alain blew out a breath and shook his head, then picked his way around the animal. Winchester immediately fell into step directly behind him.

Alain glared at the four-footed shadow. "Your dog keeps following me."

Kayla was in the living room, tending to the breakfast she was making over the fire. The other dogs were patiently standing by, waiting to be fed. She smiled over her shoulder. "I noticed. I think he's adopted you."

Just what he needed, Alain thought. "Well, tell him to unadopt me." He frowned as he made his way carefully back to the sofa. Winchester hobbled right behind him, this time trying to stay out of the way and apparently get on his good side.

Kayla transferred breakfast from the skillet to a plate, placing the former out of the way so that one of the dogs didn't accidentally pull it down.

She crossed to Alain and presented the plate of bacon and eggs to him.

"Sorry, can't make toast right now," she stated, then nodded toward Winchester, who had lain down at Alain's feet and was eyeing the plate of food wistfully. Winchester knew better than to try to snare a taste unless it was offered. "He really likes you."

Taking the plate, Alain snorted dismissively. He'd never had a pet, even as a child, and had no desire for one.

"I think he just feels guilty about making me crash my car." The moment the first forkful passed his lips, he realized just how ravenous he was. It took effort not to wolf the rest down.

Perching on the arm of the sofa, Kayla smiled tolerantly at her unexpected guest. "Dogs don't feel guilt."

"I guess that puts them one up on people." Alain thought of the case he was currently handling. His client showed absolutely no shred of guilt that her share of the inheritance cut her late husband's children completely out of the will. "At least some people," he amended.

"Everyone feels guilt," Kayla countered. Ariel nuzzled her and she absently stroked the dog's head as she spoke. "It's just a matter of whether or not they act on it."

Intrigued, Alain raised his eyes to look at her. "What do you feel guilty about?"

She hadn't expected *that* question.

"Oh." She thought a moment. Taylor tried to nudge Ariel out of the way for some attention. She gave the old dog equal time. "Not being able to do enough to save these magnificent creatures."

Alain glanced toward the fireplace, where the other dogs were still eating, then back at the two who were vying for her favor. As far as he could tell, she was already doing more than enough.

"You've got seven and a half dogs," he pointed out, throwing in the "half" because of the dog she called Ginger, who looked obviously pregnant. "How many more could you be taking in?" Without being branded eccentric, he added silently.

Her eyes swept over the animals. Alain saw the affection there and wondered why she wasn't sharing that with someone who could appreciate and reciprocate it.

"For every one I save," she told him, a thread of sadness running through her voice, "I know that two or more get euthanized."

"But you choose to focus on the positive," he asked.

"I focus on the positive," she confirmed. Otherwise, Kayla added silently, she probably wouldn't be able to make it through the day.

"What else?" he prodded.

She didn't understand what he was trying to get at. "What else what?"

She'd stirred his curiosity, making him want to know things about her. It wasn't very different from his usual approach to women, except that he felt a genuine interest in this one.

"What else do you feel guilty about? In your private life, apart from dogs. What have you done or not done that creeps up on you in the dead of night to prey on your mind and haunt you?"

That was as good a description as any she'd ever heard. *And dead-on.*

"You *are* a lawyer, aren't you?" she laughed.

Now that she'd sparked his curiosity, he wasn't about to give her a chance to turn this around. "We're talking about you, not me."

When had that happened? "No, we're not."

But even so, she reflected on his question. The only thing she felt guilty about was a time in her life when she allowed herself—in the name of love—to be bullied. She'd actually believed that if she did just what Brett wanted, they could live happily ever after. And in putting up with him, she had let everyone else down. Her parents would have expected more of her had they been alive to see what was happening.

She'd allowed her fear of being alone to back her into a corner, to tolerate the intolerable and behave like someone she wasn't.

But she'd learned. Learned that there *was* no happily ever after possible with men like Brett, nor for the people in their lives.

Kayla squared her shoulders, driving the memory away. She didn't like to think about that period of her life, didn't like thinking of herself that way—weak, submissive, constantly giving and never receiving. More than guilt, it made her feel ashamed. Ashamed and almost obsessively determined never to allow something like that to happen to her again. She had her dogs, her practice and her pledge to rescue German shepherds wherever she found them being neglected and mistreated. She didn't need a man to validate her existence, to make her feel loved.

Alain narrowed his eyes, locking them on hers. His gaze was penetrating.

"C'mon," he coaxed, and she could almost see

someone on the witness stand being mesmerized by those eyes. "There has to be something," he insisted quietly.

"Okay," she said slowly, as if was considering his question. "I feel guilty that I didn't buy that generator when I had the opportunity."

She was evading the question, Alain thought, more intrigued than ever. The more she resisted answering, the more he found himself wanting to know what it was she wasn't telling him. "I'm serious."

"So am I," she replied innocently. "Power outages happen here about twice a year. Sometimes more. If I were operating on a patient…"

Her voice trailed off. Not having a generator, now that she thought of it, was a serious oversight on her part. She needed a backup power source as much as a local hospital might. Just because her patients had four feet instead of two didn't change that. The minute the roads became passable again, she should drive to the hardware store in Everett, the neighboring town, and pick up a good generator.

She decided to turn the conversation away from her and back to him. "What about you?"

Finished eating, he placed his plate on the table. Winchester looked up at him mournfully. With a sigh, Alain nodded, and the small dog went at it.

"I never thought about getting a generator," he quipped.

Oh, no, he wasn't getting out of it that easily. "I mean what do you feel guilty about?"

"Nothing." To her ear, the response was automatic. Friendly, but with established boundaries that she could tell were not meant to be crossed.

Okay, so she wasn't allowed any further enlightenment into the mystery that was Alain Dulac. But at least her point was made. He didn't like someone prying into his life any more than she did.

But even as Kayla silently congratulated herself for not being curious enough to elbow her way into his personal life, she found herself wondering about him.

"Maybe that's why Winchester's taken to you," she said carefully, watching his expression. "He senses a kindred spirit."

Alain shook his head, not buying it. "He's looking for a handout."

Kayla's eyes dipped down to the plate on the coffee table. Everything but the rosebud design in the center of the plate had been licked off. "And he has pretty good intuition," she concluded, with an easy smile.

Alain's eyes followed her line of vision. He flushed. Winchester had cleaned the plate and was looking hopefully at him again. *That's it, dog. There ain't no more.*

"It was good," he told her, hoping she wouldn't say anything about his feeding the dog the last of the scraps. "Aren't you having any?"

She shook her head. "I tend to nibble as I cook," she told him, rising from her perch, "so technically, I've already had breakfast." Picking up the plate from the coffee table, she raised her brow in a query. "Want some coffee?"

"Please." The request was made almost worshipfully. And then he stopped. If she was offering him coffee, the stove had to have come back on. Which meant that he could use the phone to get someone to drive him home. "Is the power on?"

She wished. But she'd tested the stove just before she'd begun to make breakfast, and nothing had turned on. Kayla shook her head. "Nope."

He looked at her skeptically. "Then how are you going to make coffee?"

"Same way the cowboys used to when they were out on the range," she answered cheerfully. Kayla glanced at him over her shoulder just before she stepped into the kitchen to retrieve a battered aluminum coffeepot. "Haven't you ever been camping?"

"No." The answer was given almost defensively, as if he felt that the admission unmanned him somehow in her eyes.

Kayla stopped and looked at him incredulously. "You're kidding."

His defensiveness went up a notch. "Why would I kid about something like that?"

She shrugged nonchalantly. "No reason, I guess.

I just thought everyone went camping at some point or other in their lives." She'd pegged him right. He was a city boy, born and bred. "City kids especially, just to get away from it all."

His eyes narrowed a tad. "And by 'it' you mean electricity and flush toilets?"

She took no offense at his tone or the slight note of sarcasm in his voice. Instead, she just laughed.

The expression that came over his face was positively wicked. "My sense of adventure takes me in other directions."

For a second, her eyes met his. Kayla knew exactly what he was talking about. Unless her guess was wrong, Alain Dulac's idea of adventure involved someone of the opposite sex and a minimum of clothing.

She shook off the warm feeling that invaded her. "I'll bet," she murmured under her breath, then said audibly, "So, black?"

Okay, she'd lost him again. "Excuse me?"

"Your coffee," Kayla elaborated pleasantly. "You take it black?"

Good guess, he thought. "Yes."

"Coming up," she promised.

Kayla left the room and the dogs moved right along with her.

All except Winchester. The small shepherd with the large cast remained behind, sitting by the sofa, as if he'd been placed on guard duty. Cocking his head, he managed to move it directly beneath Alain's hand.

"Not very subtle, are you?" he laughed.

He began to pet the dog. After a beat, Winchester's rear right leg started thumping. Intrigued, Alain switched from petting to scratching. Winchester's leg responded by thumping harder, as if it had a mind of its own.

"I think your dog is about to dance a jig," Alain called out to Kayla.

Rather than shouting back, she returned with a battered coffeepot, holding the handle with an old kitchen towel she'd wrapped around it. She smiled at him, or maybe it was the dog she was smiling at.

"You found his sweet spot."

What would it take to find hers? Alain caught himself wondering. "Is that a good thing?" The leg was thumping almost frantically. He half expected the dog to fall over.

"A very good thing as far as Winchester's concerned." She peered closer at the dog's face as she came forward. "I think he's smiling."

Now she was pulling *his* leg, Alain thought. "Dogs don't smile."

"Oh, yes, they do." She said it with such conviction, he began to think that she was serious. "If my computer was up, I'd show you a whole gallery of smiling dogs." She placed the two large mugs she'd brought in with her on the coffee table, then poured what looked like liquid asphalt into each cup. Picking one up, she handed it to Alain. "Here you go. Coffee, black."

Their fingers brushed as Alain took the mug from her. He could have sworn that a spark of electricity flew between them, even if it was still conspicuously absent everywhere else.

Outside, the wind had stopped howling, but the rain continued coming down, rhythmically pelting in huge drops against the window as if it never intended to halt.

Holding the mug in both hands, Alain nodded toward the window. "How long does it generally rain here?"

"Until it stops." Kayla hid the smile that came to her lips behind her mug.

Not about to accept defeat, he tried again. "And when would that be?"

Lowering the cup, she said innocently, "When the clouds go away."

Very funny, he thought. "I can't stay here indefinitely," he told her.

"No," she agreed. "But less than twenty-four hours isn't exactly 'indefinitely.'" She knew that the laid-back answer was not the one he wanted. The man definitely needed to learn how to relax a little. She nodded toward Winchester, who hadn't moved an inch since he'd planted himself in front of Alain. "Try petting him again," she suggested. "It's a proven fact that petting a dog or cat is very soothing."

"For who?" Alain challenged, with that same note of sarcasm that seemed to come into his voice effortlessly. "The dog or cat?"

"For the human—although I'm sure the animal likes it, too." She looked at the dog closest to her—Ariel—and stroked her noble head. Ariel leaned into her hand to get the full benefit of each stroke. "Don't you, girl?"

Alain could have sworn he heard the dog sigh, but that just might have been the sound of the rain hitting the windows.

He was feeling somewhat better now, and stronger for having eaten something. He was more inclined than ever to get back on the road. "I don't want to be soothed, I need to be on my way," he told her, adding, "I've got a deposition to have transcribed, not to mention a get-together tomorrow."

"She'll wait," Kayla replied knowingly.

God knew that she herself would—if she belonged in his world, she thought, then immediately discarded the idea. Kayla had learned that this was where she belonged. Cities were all right to visit, but nothing beat the warm feeling of a town small enough that people knew your name.

"It's not a she," he told her.

"Oh." Okay, she thought, he played for the other team. Nothing wrong with that, but it did seem like an incredible waste. "Then he'll wait."

Alain knew what she was thinking—that he was in a hurry to meet someone socially. He set her straight. "I have a meeting with my boss. The whole firm is getting together. Over brunch."

She wondered if that was his firm's version of an annual picnic. "If it's over brunch, it can't be that important."

The corners of his mouth curved. Her small-town upbringing was showing. "You've never been part of the corporate world, have you?"

"No. Mercifully," she added.

But this was obviously important to him. She doubted if the car would be travel-worthy for several days.

"Tell you what. Since the lines are down, I'll take a drive later to the next town to see if Mick can come out."

"Mick?"

She was getting ahead of herself, she realized. "He's the best mechanic in two towns."

Alain wasn't naive enough to take that at face value. "Let me guess. The only mechanic in two towns."

She laughed and nodded again. "I made it too easy for you. But seriously," she stated, "Mick is good."

Alain thought back to something else she'd told him earlier. "I thought you said that the roads were impassable."

There was no discrepancy in her statements. "They are. But I know an out-of-the-way route."

As much as he wanted to be on his way, he didn't want to have this woman's demise on his conscience. "Maybe the rain'll let up."

"It always does," she allowed with a smile. "The question is how long it might take." If he was willing to wait, so much the better. "We could give it a few more hours, see what happens."

He realized he was watching her lips as she spoke. And letting his mind drift to places his gut told him she wouldn't want to go. "All right."

She moved to the other side of the sofa and fluffed the pillow. "And that'll give you more time to rest."

He did feel more tired than he was happy about, but he wasn't ready to admit that to her. "I didn't exactly exert myself lifting the fork."

"And getting dressed," she added, her eyes smiling down at him as she moved away from the sofa again. "Don't forget about getting dressed."

"Not exactly considered an Olympic event in most circles," he told her wryly.

"All depends on how challenged the dresser is," she said, amused. "You play cards?"

The question took him by surprise. He thought of

the weekly poker game Philippe held at his place. "Sure."

"Good." She crossed to the side table and opened a drawer. "Then we have a way to while away the time." Holding up a deck, she flashed him a smile.

He considered himself a damn good player. "Might not be fair," he warned her.

She winked. "I'll go easy on you."

"We are talking about poker, right?"

Sitting on the edge of the coffee table, facing him, she began to shuffle. "Is there any other game?"

"No," he agreed. "There isn't."

A few hands turned into a marathon. Except for a few breaks made necessary by little things like eating, they played well into the night. Played and talked. For Alain, time had never moved so quickly. He forgot about the rain and all the places he had to be. Where he was was far more enjoyable.

Chapter Six

The next day found Alain eager to resume playing. He was down by eight hands and he wanted to get even.

"You're down by ten," Kayla corrected, putting away the plates she'd used for their breakfast. "But who's counting?"

"You, obviously," he replied. He was feeling somewhat better today, and since it was still raining and the power was still out, playing poker kept his hands busy and his mind from straying to other activities that had an even greater allure. "C'mon, stop stalling. My ego demands that I catch up."

She knew better than that. Over the course of the hours spent playing yesterday, she'd learned that while her handsome patient enjoyed competition, he liked winning even better.

"Your ego demands that you beat me." Kayla looked amused, but then her expression became slightly somber as she scanned the room, obviously looking for something.

"What's wrong?" he asked her.

Turning around, Kayla did a quick head count. "Have you seen Ginger?"

The only name that was familiar to him was Winchester, who was still by his feet. Kayla had rattled off the other names to him yesterday, after he'd asked why she had so many dogs around. She'd told him about belonging to the German Shepherd Rescue Organization, but for the life of him, he couldn't recall the dogs' names now. "Which one's Ginger?"

She opened the hall closet. No Ginger. "The pregnant one."

"Oh, right." He couldn't recall when he'd last seen her. "I've been meaning to ask you. Why is she pregnant? I thought you'd spayed them all."

"I can't spay them all. Some I have to neuter," she teased. People confused the two terms all the time. "But to answer your question, I found her that way. With child." She walked toward the bathroom and looked in. Still no Ginger. "Or puppies, as the case may be. I wasn't about to terminate them once they were on their way."

Alain felt he had to point out the obvious. "That just means you're going to wind up with more unwanted dogs."

"I'll find people who want them," she said with confidence. "People love puppies. Just like everyone loves babies."

"Yes, but puppies grow up faster."

"By then, they've already entrenched themselves in your life and it's too late to back out." Retracing her steps, she went off in another direction, searching with no success. Where *was* that dog? "Ginger," she called as she walked out of the living room. "This is no time to play hide and seek. Get your little pregnant butt in here. Now."

Kayla's voice was growing distant as she made her way to the back of the house. And then he heard her exclaim, "Oh, damn."

He winced as he sat up straight, one hand pressed against the bandages around his ribs.

"What's wrong?" he called. "Did you find her?"

"Yes." And then he learned the reason for her dismay. "She's giving birth."

"But that's a good thing, right?" After all, Kayla was a vet. Birthing animals was part of what she did, wasn't it?

She didn't answer his question; Ginger did. A high-pitched, mournful howl pierced the air.

Gritting his teeth, Alain pushed himself up off the sofa. Winchester, who had sunk down near his feet a few minutes ago, instantly popped up, alert and ready to hobble anywhere that the man he'd surrendered his affections to was going.

"Watch your head, dog," Alain warned. He was thrown off balance as he tried his best not to trip over Winchester or step on him.

As if he understood him, the shepherd obligingly took a step back, out of the way.

Coincidence, Alain thought. Steadier now, he followed the sound of the howling. It led him to the kitchen, where he found Ginger scrunched up beneath a rectangular table. She wasn't alone. Kayla was right beside her.

"Anything I can do to help?" he offered a little uncertainly. "Aren't dogs supposed to do this by themselves? They've been doing it since the beginning of time, long before there were vets to tend to them."

"So have women," she countered. "Squatting in the field and giving birth, then going on with whatever farm chore they were doing before they went into labor. But most women do a lot better with help instead of going it alone, don't you think?"

She wasn't about to get an argument from him about that, he decided. His brother Georges was a doctor. Still, Alain was hard-pressed to try to visualize the German shepherd taking deep breaths and panting in between pushes—although now that he noticed, she did seem to have the panting down pat.

Trying not to pay attention to the pain radiating from his ribs, he squatted down to be face level with Kayla. "What do you want me to do?"

It was on the tip of her tongue to say, "Stay out of the way," because there was only so much room beneath the table. Besides, if he exerted himself he might wind up making his own condition that much worse. There was no way she would be able to attend to Ginger and help him at the same time.

But one look at Alain's face told her that he was sincere. Maybe he could save her a few steps, she decided. That seemed harmless enough.

"If you could get the basin that's under the sink for me, rinse it out and fill it with warm water, I would appreciate it." The second she mentioned the temperature, she remembered. With the power out, the water heater wasn't working. "Oh, damn, there isn't any warm water," she amended. There was only one thing to do. "Well, fill it with cold water—and towels. I need towels," she told him. Glancing over her shoulder at him, she could see his next question forming. "There are clean kitchen towels in the cabinet right next to the sink." She pointed in that direction.

Placing a hand on top of the table, Alain drew

himself up. It took him a couple of seconds to locate the cabinet she was referring to. When he opened it, he saw that it was stuffed with towels.

"How many?"

"Two, three, whatever you can grab."

It was happening, Kayla thought. The miracle. Ginger was ready to give birth. She didn't care how common it was or how often it happened before her eyes, it was still a miracle, each and every time. But even miracles needed a helping hand every now and then.

"Hurry," she told him.

"Hurrying," Alain assured her.

He grabbed a handful of clean towels from the cabinet and brought them over to Kayla as fast as he was able.

There was a large damp spot on the floor beneath the table and he could have sworn he saw something emerging from Ginger's nether region, accompanied by a low, moaning noise.

He glanced at Kayla for confirmation. "Is that—?"

She didn't wait for him to finish. The puppies were definitely coming. "Yes. Basin. Water." The words shot out like bullets. Her eyes were riveted on the animal in labor.

By the time he got the basin filled—and avoided colliding with his four-footed, furry shadow—Alain saw that Kayla had a tiny, scrawny, hairless bit of life in her hands. It looked more like a little rat than a puppy.

"That's what they look like when they're born?" he asked incredulously.

She could tell by his tone that he found the puppy less than appealing. *Pagan.*

"Yes," she said, carefully drying the tiny black puppy. "Beautiful."

When he looked at the newly minted animal, it wasn't the first descriptive word that occurred to him. Or the second. But Alain had a feeling that was something best kept to himself.

"There's another one!" he cried, watching a second puppy emerge.

His reaction tickled her. "Where there's smoke…" She allowed her voice to trail off as she took possession of the second puppy, also black, and wiped him clean. She set both puppies down beside her.

They continued coming like clockwork, one after the other. Twenty minutes later, there were nine of them.

"Is that it?" he asked her, amazed that so many puppies had come out of a relatively small German shepherd.

"I think so."

He heard something in her voice. A note of distress he hadn't heard before. "What is it?"

"This one isn't breathing." The last puppy, the tiniest one of the lot, lay still in her hand.

"Isn't there something you can do?" he asked. It seemed wrong, somehow, to mar this celebration of birth with a death at the same time.

Holding the puppy in her hand, its spine resting against her palm, Kayla began to gently massage the tiny chest. Ever so delicately, she blew into the puppy's nostrils. It was all she could think of. This had never happened to her before. With all the litters she'd delivered, there had never been a stillborn.

She didn't want there to be one now.

"Here," Alain offered, "let me try. My hands are bigger."

As if that made a difference.

Kayla wanted to ask him what he thought he could do that she couldn't, but she knew how agonizing the futility of facing death could be. So she handed over the puppy and watched Alain do exactly what she had been doing—but less gently and with more vigor.

"That's not going to—" She was going to tell him to stop when she saw the slight movement. The puppy's chest had moved. And again. Stunned, she looked up at Alain. "He's breathing. The puppy's breathing."

Alain grinned. "Yeah, I know. I can feel it in my hand." He looked down at the small creature in his palm. "Almost lost you there, didn't we?" He felt a sense of triumph, a rush that he'd never experienced before, even when winning a case in court. There was something pure and unadulterated about being part of bringing a life into the world.

Kayla smiled, touched by the way he'd responded to the puppy, and impressed by the way he'd responded to the emergency.

Alain glanced up and saw how she was looking at him. Again he was aware of the crackle of electricity between them. But this time, it felt softer, more intimate.

Rousing herself, Kayla looked down at Ginger and stroked the dog's head. "You did good, Mama. Now it's time to feed your babies."

Alain was still on his knees, and he helped her round up the small, wobbly litter. There were nine tiny puppies in need of sustenance, vying for position at a bar where only eight could be seated at any one time.

Holding the puppy he'd saved, and another one against him, Alain raised his eyes toward Kayla. "She's only got, um, eight…" He was really out of his element here, he thought.

Kayla grinned. "Nothing gets by you, does it?" Rising to her feet, she crossed to another cupboard. When she turned around again, he saw that she had an empty baby bottle in her hand. She filled it with milk from the refrigerator and then crawled back under the table, next to him.

Alain had gently ushered eight of the puppies toward their first meal, and they were doing the rest. She noted that he was still holding the puppy he'd breathed life into. Kayla offered the bottle to him. She would have preferred warming the milk, but this would have to do for now.

"Want to do the honors?" she asked.

He glanced at the bottle and then the puppy. It didn't really look like a good fit; the bottle seemed almost as large as the puppy. The tiny creature was mewling, sounding more like a kitten than a canine.

Taking the bottle, he looked at Kayla. "He'll drink this?"

"Why don't you put the nipple near his mouth and see?" she suggested.

He had no idea why her innocent words conjured up the image within his head that it did. An image that had far less to do with nourishing a puppy and a great deal more with nourishing something within him. It took him a couple of moments to clear the picture from his mind.

Nodding, he said, "Okay."

The second he brought the nipple to the puppy's mouth, the newborn began sucking madly, as if starving.

Alain smiled at the way the puppy ate with such

gusto. And then he realized something. "His eyes are shut."

Kayla nodded, watching over the other eight even as she kept glancing over her shoulder at Alain and the puppy he was feeding. "That's how they come, wiggly, hairless and sightless." She continued to stroke Ginger's head. "Something only a mother could love," she added softly.

"And you."

Her eyes met his. She smiled and something stirred inside of him. "And me," she agreed.

Outside, the wind howled and the rain lashed at the windows again, as if unleashing round two. Caught up in the miracle of the moment, neither one of them noticed.

"Where are you going?"

It was several hours later. Ginger and her brood had been moved over by the fireplace to keep them all warm. Alain had spent most of his time watching over the new mother and her puppies. Winchester had placed himself in close proximity to both man and new mother. Winchester was there, at Alain's feet. Ginger tolerated him. As for Alain, he was amused by the microdynamics of this small society.

Kayla's crossing to the front door, a rain slicker draped over her clothes, instantly roused him from this uncomplicated, domestic scene. Was she going out in weather like this?

She fished out the keys to her truck. "I'm going to see about getting Mick to come out and at least take a look at your car, see if it can be salvaged."

The birthing process and the business of caring for Ginger and the new puppies—especially Nine, which was what he'd called the one he'd saved—seemed so surreal it had knocked out all sense of time. He felt like he was someplace where the minutes just stood still. But the mention of his car brought reality—and his shot-to-hell schedule—back to Alain.

"And if it can't?" he asked. "Is there a car-rental agency around here?"

She smiled. "You might be able to pay Mick or one of his people to drive you wherever you have to go—once the weather clears up a little."

Alain groaned. That didn't sound promising. From where he sat, it looked like the kind of weather in which a man with a flowing beard would feel called upon to collect two of everything and push them onto his boat.

"How long do you think that'll be?"

Kayla shook her head as she raised her hood to cover her hair. "Haven't a clue," she confessed. "It doesn't usually rain at all this time of year." About to walk out, she hesitated, then looked at him over her shoulder. "There's dry dog food in the garage if you want to bribe any of them. I'm taking Taylor and Ariel, but the rest are staying with you."

He looked uneasily at the dogs she was leaving behind. There were three besides Winchester and Ginger. Not counting the puppies. He couldn't help feeling vastly outnumbered.

"You think that's wise? I'm a stranger to them."

Not after forty-eight hours, she thought. The number struck her. Had it really only been that long? It certainly felt longer.

"The dogs are smart. They can sense things. They know you're not here to steal the silverware." She grinned. He still looked somewhat uncertain. "I'll be back as soon as I can," she promised.

"Sure the phones aren't working?" he called after her.

Instead of leaving, Kayla doubled back to the kitchen. Picking up the receiver from the wall unit, she held it toward him without saying a word. Even with the distance between them, he could hear that there was nothing but silence coming from the receiver.

"I'm sure," she said. Then she smiled at him, resurrecting that same odd tightening inside his gut. As she passed him, she patted his shoulder. Much the way, he noted, that she'd stroked Ginger's head. "You'll be fine," she assured him.

And then she was gone.

* * *

He kept checking his watch, wondering if Kayla was all right. Shouldn't she have gotten back by now? It felt like an eternity since she'd left.

Where was she?

As a lawyer, he was worried that something might have happened to her in the storm, and since he'd sent her out, he was liable for her. He could be sued on a number of counts if she—or her estate— were savvy enough to think like lawyers. As a man, he just worried about her welfare and wanted her back, safe and sound. And presiding over her dogs. He didn't feel too comfortable about the way two of them had begun pacing. Did they know something he didn't?

Or were they just doing that to intimidate him?

He hadn't a clue.

Each time he rose to his feet, whether to look out the window or to get something from the refrigerator, he couldn't shake the sensation of having five pairs of eyes trained on him. Even the puppies seemed to raise their heads in the direction of the sound he made. Definitely unnerving.

When Kayla finally walked through the door, the five dogs who rushed to her were not the only ones who were happy to see her. Walking across the threshold, she shed her slicker and sent a mini-shower onto the floor as she laughed at the greeting, petting two dogs at a time.

"How were they?" she asked, looking at the puppies.

"They survived my care," he answered. He noticed that aside from the two dogs Kayla had taken with her, she was alone. "Couldn't get him to come, I take it?"

Kayla looked at Alain quizzically for a second before she realized who he was asking about. "Oh, you mean Mick. Yes, I got him to come."

"And he's where, in your pocket?"

"No, he's outside, looking over your car." The rain had subsided a bit, no longer coming down at an all-but-blinding rate.

Alain crossed to her, not bothering to hide his eagerness. What he did hide was that he still felt incredibly achy.

"And?"

"And he's outside, looking over your car," she repeated. Alain lived in a faster-paced world than she did, where everything was done yesterday. She'd sampled that world, and been more than happy to leave it behind when she came back here. "That's all I know for now."

He was pushing, Alain realized. He'd been driven all his adult life, and it wasn't something he could easily brush off. "Sorry, I'm not usually this antsy."

He didn't want her thinking of him as another man who lived in the fast lane. Why, he wasn't sure.

Kayla inclined her head. "This isn't exactly your typical, run-of-the-mill situation," she admitted.

Crouching, she quickly looked over the puppies, just to satisfy her own concerns. To her delight, they really were fine. These she could find a home for. As she'd told Alain before she left, everyone loved puppies.

Before he could agree with her assessment, he heard the front door opening again. Turning, he saw a tall thin man, with long, dirty-blond hair—currently wet—walk in. The smell of oil and gasoline followed him. Small, intent brown eyes looked him over before the man finally offered his hand.

"Mick Hollister," he introduced himself. "Pretty fancy car for these parts."

Alain derived his own interpretation from the man's words. It wasn't admiration so much as a lack of knowledge in the man's voice. Disappointment reared. "Then you can't fix it."

"Oh, I can fix it, all right," Mick assured him. "They haven't invented a machine I can't fix. But it's gonna take awhile," he warned Alain. "Gotta get parts, that kind of stuff. Not something I usually stock."

Alain could see this stretching out to two, three weeks. And as much as he found himself liking this feisty vet's company, he needed to get back. "I don't have awhile."

Mick nodded, absorbing the information. Keeping his judgments simple. "Then I guess you've got a problem."

Alain was nothing if not a problem solver. Maybe not as good as Philippe, but he could hold his own. "How about if I leave the car with you to be fixed, and meanwhile, you drive me to Orange County?" He could see that the other man was not keen on the idea. "I'll pay you."

But Mick shook his head. "Sorry, can't leave my shop. Too much work to do," he explained.

Alain couldn't see much money being made in a small town like this, or the neighboring vicinity. "I'll pay you twice whatever it is you're making working on the cars."

Instead of jumping at the chance the way he thought the mechanic might, the older man shook his head. "That wouldn't be right. I'd be robbing you."

Alain had never run into honesty as a stumbling block before. In his line of work, the opposite was usually the case. Stunned, he looked at Kayla. "He's serious."

"As a thunderstorm," she replied simply. She picked up Nine and stroked him as she spoke. "Is there anyone you can call to come pick you up— once the phone lines are back up?"

He sighed, frustrated. There were his brothers and several cousins he could call—if he could call. Which he couldn't in this backward town. He was stuck, he thought. Alain didn't think that anyone would miss him until some time next week, when he had to file papers regarding another case he was handling. He doubted that Rachel would call either of his brothers to say he hadn't shown up for their date, or that anyone from his office would think to check why he had missed the meeting and wasn't in the office today. Which left him as stranded as the Prisoner of Zenda.

"Yes," he finally said, "there are several people I could call—if I could call," he repeated. "How long before the lines are back up?"

Kayla shrugged casually. "Hard to say. On the average, it's not more than a few days."

A few days. That translated to an eternity in his world.

As if sensing his agitation, Winchester hobbled next to him, planted himself on his rear and looked up at him adoringly while his tail moved back and forth like a deranged metronome.

"If I were you, mister, I'd just relax and make the best of it," Mick suggested. And then he followed his words with what sounded like a wicked laugh.

Alain couldn't help noticing that the man with the dirt-stained fingers had deliberately looked toward Kayla as he tendered his advice.

Chapter Seven

Outside, it was growing dark. The rain had finally stopped, but the sky looked ominous, as if another storm was in the making. And the power still had not made an appearance.

Alain was stranded, which ordinarily would make him agitated. Not having control over something usually did that to him. Yet as he sat at the kitchen table with the candles casting elongated shadows about the room, he felt calm inside. Since he couldn't do anything to change the situation, he'd come to terms with it.

After all, the power outage couldn't last forever.

At least he hoped not. And rather than get frustrated because he couldn't do anything about it, he made himself relax and take in the moment.

And the woman who was so much a part of it.

Right now, Kayla was busy getting their dinner ready. He'd offered to help, but she had told him just to sit and relax, that too many people milling about the fireplace would get in each other's way. He assumed that "two" constituted "too many."

So here he sat, watching her.

And he liked watching her.

Alain's mind drifted back to his situation. He doubted if he'd be replaced on the case he was currently assigned to at the firm. Bobbie Jo Halliday liked him, and money talked. Besides, it really hadn't been *that* long. Maybe by tomorrow the power would be restored, and, more importantly, the phones lines would rise up from the dead.

Periodically he'd take his cell phone out of his pocket and check to see if it was finally receiving some sort of signal. Every time he flipped it open, the tiny screen gave him the same message: *Searching for a network.*

Obviously the network had decided to take a holiday.

The mechanic that Kayla had brought back with her was long gone. Mick had taken Alain's BMW back to "the shop," wherever that was.

It occurred to Alain that he was placing a great deal of trust in this woman he hadn't even known existed seventy-two hours ago. Maybe that was a mistake.

He thought of some of the mysteries—his favorite form of entertainment—that he'd read. What if this Mick character was really stealing his car? And he was stripping it in order to sell the vehicle for parts. Kayla could be in on it, she could even—

Alain reined in his thoughts. The woman was not the devious, mastermind type. She was—

Suddenly he felt something wet and rough against the back of his hand and fingers. He looked down to see that Winchester had made his way over again and was licking his hand.

Alain didn't bother restraining the smile that rose to his lips. He'd even begun to feel a small measure of affection for the injured dog—one injured creature relating to another, he mused.

The stew she'd put together had been simmering nicely and, if the dissolving diced potatoes were any indication, it looked as if it was finally done. Time to eat.

Kayla glanced over her shoulder toward the kitchen and Alain.

She smiled fondly at Winchester. Her smile took in Alain, as well. "He's just trying to get you to pay attention to him." She wasn't sure, but she thought she saw Alain raise a quizzical eyebrow. "He thinks you've been won over by Nine and his crew."

"I haven't been 'won over' by anything," Alain protested, although, reflecting back, he had to admit that saving the last puppy had been a rather emotional experience.

Kayla moved away from the fireplace, dusting off her hands on the back of her jeans. The grin on her face as she spared him another look told Alain that she knew otherwise.

She made her way to the cupboard and took down two large bowls. "Oh, I think you have. Nothing wrong with having a soft spot in your heart for animals—dogs especially."

She began to ladle out equal portions of stew. Taylor and Ariel took an extreme interest in her every move, anticipating a handout. She deliberately avoided making eye contact with the dogs.

Kayla brought both bowls to the table and set them down. Turning, she went to another cabinet and retrieved a bottle of wine, then two glasses.

"Didn't you have a favorite pet when you were growing up?"

He waited for her to sit down opposite him before picking up his fork. The stew smelled incredible and he could feel his appetite spiking.

In more ways than one, he thought, watching as

she pushed her hair back out of her eyes. He took a sip of wine.

"I didn't have a pet," he answered, "favorite or otherwise."

She raised her eyes to his. Even in this dim light, he thought they were mesmerizing. "You're kidding."

Alain forced himself to look down at his dinner and not at her. He took another sip of wine before responding. A warm, mellow feeling began to slip over him. "Why would I kid about that?"

When she gave no answer, he raised his eyes to her face. She was looking at him as if she'd suddenly realized how deprived he was.

"I'm sorry," she told him softly.

He wasn't sure he followed her. "Sorry you thought I was kidding?"

"No, sorry that you didn't have a pet." He'd missed out on a lot, she thought. "Everyone should have at least one pet in their lives." She looked over to where Ginger was lying, her puppies in a semicircle around her. Kayla's sweeping glance took in the other dogs, as well, ending with Winchester, who was standing at Alain's left like a small, furry bodyguard. "There's nothing like the feeling of having a set of adoring brown eyes looking up at you."

Alain laughed before he could think better of it and stop himself. Her description pretty much summed up the way Rachel always looked up at him—he was almost a foot taller than she was. The woman had to have the softest eyes he'd ever seen. That is, they had been until he'd looked down at Winchester.

"You're thinking of your girlfriend, aren't you?" Kayla asked.

The knowing tone, breaking into his thoughts, took him by surprise. Without thinking, he dropped his left hand and began to stroke Winchester's head. A peacefulness seeped into him.

"How did you know what I was thinking about?" he challenged.

That was easy, she thought as she swallowed another forkful of her stew. "You smirked."

"No, I didn't," he protested, then realized he was becoming defensive when there was no reason to. He liked Rachel, but there wasn't anything lasting between them. Just as there had never been anything lasting between him and any of the other women he took out. He couldn't get serious about a woman. He wouldn't allow it. "And besides, I wouldn't call her my girlfriend."

So there was a "her" in his life, Kayla thought. Finding that out shouldn't have made a difference, one way or another. The fact that it bothered her both intrigued and worried her.

She did what she could to bank down her feelings.

"Then what would you call her?" she asked mildly, aware that she was marginally flirting with him and enjoying it.

He shrugged his shoulders. It felt a little strange discussing his personal life with this woman. Especially since he was having difficulty drawing his eyes away from her. "Rachel."

Rachel. Pretty name. Probably a very pretty girl. Why did that even matter? "Does this Rachel know she's not your girlfriend?"

"Yes," he answered firmly. In case Kayla was casting him in the role of some heartless womanizer, he added with feeling, "I don't make a secret of how I feel about relationships."

This was getting very, very interesting. "And how do you feel about relationships?"

Alain narrowed his eyes as he looked at her. "What are you, my shrink?"

She countered with another mild question. "Do you have one?"

His question had been intentionally sarcastic, not intended as some sort of revelation. He didn't believe in baring his soul to a stranger.

Then what the hell are you doing right now?

Alain frowned. "No."

"Then, no," Kayla replied whimsically, looking back at her dinner, "I'm not."

Winchester was nudging him. Alain fished out a

bit of meat from his bowl and offered it to the dog. No sooner was it in his hand than it was gone. Winchester's teeth had never even touched his skin.

"Why all the questions?" he asked.

Kayla's expression when she looked up at him was innocence personified. "It's called conversation, Alain. You might have noticed, the radio and TV are out and talking is the only form of entertainment that's left to us at the moment. We did it last night over cards. Why can't we do it over dinner?" She shifted slightly in her seat, ignoring the begging animals on either side of her. The other dogs knew better than to beg, but Taylor and Ariel were her newest charges, and they were still hopeful. "Now, unless you'd rather just sit there like a statue, it's your turn to answer." She could see by his expression that she'd lost him in the maze of words. "You were going to tell me how you felt about relationships."

"No, I wasn't."

She leaned forward a little, and a soft, sensual fragrance tickled his nose. Moved his soul. "Humor me. I saved your life."

Alain made a show of trying to hold his ground, all the while knowing that he'd answer her in the end. "People don't die from cracked ribs."

"They do if the rib punctures a lung," she countered, growing serious for a moment. "Now you really have me curious," she admitted, still sitting on the edge of her seat. "You're obviously against relationships. Why?" Could it be for the same reason that she'd been steering clear of men these last couple of years? "Did someone hurt you, Alain?"

The woman was getting way too personal, and yet he couldn't bring himself to tell her that. Maybe because there was something almost surreal about being trapped here like this, in the middle of a storm, he allowed himself to purge his soul. This place would be in his past soon, as if it had never existed.

"No," he told her and it was the truth. He'd never allowed anyone the chance to hurt him. Because his mother had taught him that, by example.

Kayla wasn't sure if she quite believed him. "Then you're just a carefree, confirmed bachelor?"

Finished eating, Alain moved the bowl away from the edge of the table and Winchester's wistful gaze. "Something like that."

She paused for a moment, studying his face. And then she shook her head. "You're too young to be a confirmed anything."

She kept surprising him. "How do you know how old I am?"

Kayla shrugged carelessly, avoiding his eyes. "Your driver's license."

"You looked at my driver's license?"

She raised her head, looking at him as if she hadn't done anything out of the ordinary.

"While you were unconscious. I like knowing who I'm dragging into my house." Then, because he was still frowning, she added, "You could have been a serial killer."

"They don't put that on driver's licenses," he pointed out.

"True," she allowed, "but I did learn your name. And if you were wanted for anything, I'd know."

He didn't see how. "Are you one of those police program junkies?"

Watching *Cops* was a guilty pleasure she allowed herself, but judging from his tone, he looked down on things like that. So she said, "I wouldn't go so far as calling myself a junkie—I just like being informed, and I make myself aware of who's wanted for a crime."

He decided there was no point in arguing about what Kayla had done. Instead, he turned it to his benefit. "Okay, so you know my age. How old are you?"

"A gentleman never asks that of a lady," she countered smoothly.

The woman had more moves than a welterweight champion. "I'm just looking for a trade of information here."

She reconsidered. "Fair enough, I suppose. I'm twenty-seven."

She looked younger, he thought. "Ever been married?"

"No." Her eyes held his as she asked, "You?"

He thought they'd covered that when she asked about relationships. Was she intentionally trying to trip him up? "No. Siblings?"

"None. You?"

He thought of Philippe and Georges, both now settled. Unlike him. It seemed to him as if the dynamics in his life had changed rather quickly. "I've got two brothers."

"You're lucky."

The longing in her voice was hard to miss. He wouldn't have traded positions with an only child for the world, even though there had been knock-down, drag-out fights in his past, mostly with Georges. "At times," he allowed.

She envied his memories. If she'd had siblings, maybe Brett would have never been in her life, would have never had a chance to upend it the way he had. "Parents still alive?"

The way she phrased it told him that hers weren't. "Just my mother."

Kayla caught the inflection in his voice. Finished eating, she pushed her bowl away and leaned her elbow on the table, her chin on her palm. Humor curved her mouth. "What is it about your mother that makes you roll your eyes?"

For a second, he thought of brushing off her question, but then, he was no longer embarrassed by his mother. Certainly not the way he'd been when he was growing up, and her free-wheeling lifestyle had mortified him. As an adult, he could understand his mother's quest to have someone in her life who would adore her. And he understood her fickleness.

"My mother is Lily Moreau." Even as he told Kayla, he had his doubts she would recognize the name. This wasn't exactly the hub of culture.

One look at Kayla's face told him he'd guessed wrong. A skeptical look had entered her eyes. "Lily Moreau is your mom?"

He couldn't tell by her tone if she liked or disliked his mother. Something protective stirred in his chest. All of them had grown protective of Lily.

"Yes."

He was pulling her leg, Kayla thought. But if that was his intent, wouldn't he have used someone more famous, less controversial? "Lily Moreau, the artist."

"You've heard of her."

Now *that* she took offense at. "This isn't Brigadoon. We're small, but we're only about a hundred and twenty miles from L.A. County. We get *People* magazine around here, and next month," she told him brightly, "they say we might even get indoor plumbing."

He'd insulted her, he realized. "Sorry."

Kayla ignored the apology, more taken with the information he'd just given her. She'd seen photographs of the famous woman. The handsome blond man at Kayla's table didn't look a thing like the raven-haired artist.

"She's really your mother," she said again, disbelief lingering in her voice.

"I'll e-mail you a photograph of the two of us when I get home if you want proof." And then, because he'd been toying with the thought of seeing her again, he said, "Better yet, if you come down, I'll introduce you." He knew he had to qualify that, in case Kayla took him up on the invitation. His mother was nothing if not unpredictable. "Provided that she's in town. She has a habit of taking off and flying around the world on a moment's notice." At least, it had always seemed that way to him. "Though not as much as she used to."

Because she admired strong, independent women, Kayla knew more than a little about the famous artist. "What's it like, having such a famous mother?"

When he had been very young, it had bothered Alain that his mother was always taking off, that she wasn't like the mothers his friends had. But over the years, he'd made his peace with that. These days, now that he understood her better, he was rather proud of what she had accomplished. A lot of women would have surrendered in defeat, especially after their husband had practically sold the house out from under them—as Philippe's father had, to fund his gambling addiction.

"Apart from sharing her with the world, it has its moments," he murmured succinctly.

He was holding something back, Kayla thought. She tried to read between the lines. "You must have had an interesting childhood, traveling all over the globe, wherever there was an art gallery."

He'd wanted to, but Philippe had always been the voice of reason, pointing out that the trips would get in the way of Alain's schooling. He'd hated his brother for that. And hated his mother for listening. Now, Alain was grateful. He wouldn't be where he was if it hadn't been for Philippe.

"Not really. Most of the time, we stayed home, wherever home was at the time."

Philippe and even Georges had gone through more turmoil than he had. With each new husband, a new return address would appear in the corner of the envelope. As far as touring the different art galleries, he and the others remained home, technically under the care of nannies. But it was really Philippe who took care of them, Philippe who had handled the assignment his mother unwittingly thrust on him: being his brothers' keeper and surrogate father.

"Is that why you don't have relationships?" Kayla asked suddenly. "Because of your mother?"

The question caught him off guard, and hit much too close to home. "I thought you said you were a vet, not a head doctor."

She shrugged. "In a small town, you get to stretch beyond your boundaries, be a little of everything."

"I don't belong in this town," he reminded her. Which negated her right to analyze him.

Kayla didn't back away. "You're here now. That's all that matters."

She made it sound like a life sentence. He took it a step further. "You mentioned Brigadoon. If I'm here past midnight, does that mean I have to stay for the next hundred years?"

"Maybe you hit your head harder than I thought," she said. Getting up, she rounded the table and went through the motions of looking for a bump on his head. "You've already stayed here over night," she pointed out. "In fact, you're going on three."

She was standing so close to him, Alain could feel the heat coming from her body. Could feel the urges being aroused in his own.

All he had to do, he thought, was reach up and pull her down to his lap.

And kiss her.

He wanted to kiss her in the worst way, he finally admitted to himself. And something told him that if he did, she'd be receptive. But if he kissed Kayla, it would mean something to her. He doubted if he was ready for that. If he'd *ever* be ready for that.

But he still wanted to kiss her.

"Just a joke," he told her, turning his head to look at her. Brushing his arm against her leg.

"Oh." Kayla inhaled sharply when his eyes touched hers.

She shouldn't have put that bottle of wine out, she told herself. Or she shouldn't have had any of it. Wine always did things to her. Made her vulnerable as well as exceedingly fluid. She felt as if she could easily melt into his hands if he touched her.

Then why aren't you backing away? Why are you just standing here, waiting for him to reach for you?

Rousing herself, Kayla took a step back. Or tried to. It felt as if she were trying to walk through glue.

And then he did it. Hands bracketing her hips, Alain drew her onto his lap.

"You shouldn't be doing this," she warned. When he looked at her, waiting for her to elaborate, she told him, "You could hurt yourself."

He laughed. "You don't weigh that much."

"I wasn't thinking about weight," she replied. "A man in heat doesn't always think straight, and you do have cracked ribs."

He slowly ran his thumb along her lower lip. A thrill of anticipation ran through him, leaving no part untouched. He felt as if his whole body had suddenly gone on alert.

"It's a kiss, Kayla," he whispered softly, "just a kiss, nothing more."

Her breath was already caught in her throat. "You never know how these things will turn out," she stated, barely aware that the words were leaving her lips.

Get off his lap, something inside her cried. *Now. Before it's too late.*

But it was already too late.

Chapter Eight

It was too late, because his lips had found and captured hers.

Too late, because her body was already melting into a sizzling puddle.

Too late, because she was responding. Responding to him, to the kiss, with such intensity that had she had any breath to spare, it would have been sucked away immediately.

As it was, she was swiftly becoming light-headed even as she felt her pulse racing faster than the lead car at the Indianapolis 500.

She could no longer remember when she'd last been kissed by a man, or kissed one back.

She was kissing back now.

It was as if every single logical process that went on in her mind had suddenly opted to take a holiday.

She was melting faster than a handful of snow in the month of July.

Kayla wrapped her arms around Alain's neck and lost her way.

Lost herself in the heat, in the anticipation. In the excitement that leaped through her veins.

Damn, but he was a good kisser.

The best she'd ever had by a long shot. She found herself grateful to Brett and his mean streak. Had he not had one, she would have never found herself here, going up in smoke and thrilled about it. She would have gone on thinking that Brett was as good as it got.

She would have been so wrong.

Alain deepened the kiss, amazed at the sensations he was feeling. He wasn't drunk—it took far more than two glasses of wine for that to happen—but he certainly felt drunk. And drugged. And wildly aroused.

This feisty little vet with the soft lips made his heart race and the air in his lungs all but disappear.

Trying to get his bearings, he cupped her face in his hands and gently drew back so that he could look at her.

His eyes caressed her. "We're not in Kansas anymore," he murmured.

"Not even in Oz," she whispered back, surprised that her lips worked. She'd been fairly certain they'd been singed off.

Alain fought the very real, very strong temptation to go on kissing her. His palms itched and he wanted nothing more than to touch her, to trace the outline of her body with his fingertips and memorize each curve, each contour.

Hell, he wanted everything. Wanted to make love with her until he was too numb to move. She was turning him inside out and he was willingly allowing it to happen.

Alain drew in a long, deep breath. "We seem to have a new development here." His mouth suddenly felt so dry, he might have been gargling with sand.

She didn't want to hear about it, didn't want to hear about logic, or pause to weigh and measure consequences. Didn't want to think at all. She just wanted this to continue to its rightful conclusion. Otherwise, she was going to burn up in frustration.

"Stop being a lawyer," she told him, her voice low and husky.

Before Alain could reply, she was kissing him again, slanting her mouth against his over and over to prevent the parade of words from escaping. Kayla wasn't interested in his philosophies or his ability to reason things out. Wasn't interested in his legal mind or his rhetoric. What she was interested in was having the wild rush in her veins continue. She wanted him to kiss the hollow of her neck and make her crazy with desire.

Okay, crazier.

"Yes, ma'am."

She felt rather than heard his response, felt his smile ripple against her skin as he pressed his lips to her throat.

She moaned and gave herself up wholeheartedly to the feeling.

Somewhere during the heated, moist tangle of tongues, lips and teeth, Alain slowly rose to his feet. In sync with him, Kayla slid off his lap and planted her feet on the floor. Arms still entwined around his neck, she pressed herself against him.

She sucked in her breath and reveled in his hard, firm body. Her very core felt as if it were on fire. It took everything she had not to just leap up into his arms and wrap her legs around his waist. But in Alain's bruised condition, that could only hurt him.

Yet it was oh so hard to be reasonable when she burned like this.

Kayla didn't know which of them started the process first—whether she began tugging his clothes off or he hers. All she knew was that clothing began piling up on the floor beside the table as items were stripped off, one by one.

With each, her body temperature went up a degree, until she felt utterly fevered. And nude.

And then momentarily airborne. Alain caught her up in his arms and lifted her onto the table.

"Your ribs," she protested. She didn't want him reinjuring himself.

Ever so gently, he pushed her down on the table. The main course for his feast.

"You taped them up damn well," he told her, just before he began to conduct a complete inventory of her body. He covered every single inch first with his hands, then his lips.

She twisted beneath him, absorbing every touch, aching for more.

Kayla could feel the scream of pleasure bubbling up in her throat, and pressed her lips together as hard as she could. Any sudden cry from her could be misconstrued and instantly bring at least six dogs to her rescue, if not Ginger, too. They were very protective of her. She was taking no chances on Alain getting hurt—or the delicious assault on her body being halted.

Climaxes were rocking her, one exquisitely flowering into another as she arched against his mouth. But even as her head swam and she craved more, her sense of fair play broke through. It didn't seem right for this to be so one-sided.

Drawing on a great deal of strength, she raised her head to look at him. "What about you?" she panted.

Busy tracing a warm, moist trail between her thighs, Alain glanced up at her. She'd never seen a more sensually wicked look than the one on his face.

"I'm doing fine," he assured her. As he spoke, his breath brushed against her skin, all but driving her to the brink of distraction.

Another climax exploded within her.

She was swiftly losing the last shred of rationality and didn't want that to happen until they came together.

With superhuman effort, Kayla pushed herself up to a sitting position and then slid off the table. Before he could ask if she'd changed her mind, she wrapped her fingers possessively around his and tugged him down to the floor.

"I want you," she murmured thickly.

It was all he needed to hear. All he wanted to hear. The next moment, they were lost in each other's arms as he kissed her again. Kissed her as if he'd never done it before.

Kissed her until she felt her very soul leaping for joy.

And then, her back flat against the floor, his mouth sealed to hers, he entered her. They were joined, becoming one, instantly moving to a shared rhythm that they both felt beating within their chests.

They climbed together, faster and faster, until suddenly streamers of starlight burst over them.

Gripped by a feeling of euphoria, Kayla hung on to the afterglow as long as she could. Then he was pivoting his weight onto his elbows as he looked down into her face.

He was smiling.

"Something funny?" Her effort not to sound breathless was a failure. She wasn't expecting the answer that he gave her.

"Life," Alain told her. "If I'd paid for Halliday's valet to come down to L.A. to give his deposition, instead of driving to him, I'd never been caught in this storm, never wrecked my BMW." His fingers feathered along her cheek, moving a strand of hair away so that he could look at her unobstructed. She thought he was lamenting the events he was citing, until he added, "And I would have never been saved by you."

The way he said it made it seem as if he was talking about more than just her dragging him from the vehicle.

She was reading too much into it, Kayla decided. It was all just wishful thinking on her part, nothing more. Everyone knew that fantastic lovers did not make faithful lovers. It was a law written some-where.

The next moment, his body still pressed to hers, Alain jerked and stiffened.

Her eyes widened. "What's the matter?"

He laughed and then pointed behind him. Taylor was standing there, looming very close to his posterior. "I've just been goosed. I think he's jealous." And then he looked at her, his expression growing serious. "I think maybe we should take this to your bedroom."

"You want to do it again?"

Alain couldn't tell by her expression if his suggestion appalled her. Until this second, he'd thought that the pleasure was mutual. "It wasn't that bad, was it?"

"Bad?" Is that what he thought? She was quick to set him straight. "No. Oh, God, no. It's just that…" How could she put this without sounding as if she slept around? "I thought men could only do it once a night."

His smile was amused, and somehow still managed to seem incredibly intimate to her. "Lady, you've had the wrong lovers."

Lovers. Did he think she had sex casually? Well, what else would he think? They hadn't exactly known each other from the first grade, had they? He hadn't been in her life three days, and here they were, making love. So what did that make her?

Incredibly glad, a small voice whispered in her head.

When Alain extended his hand, she wrapped her fingers around it and allowed him to help her to her feet. Her knees didn't quite feel solid at the moment.

* * *

They made love two more times. Each time felt as exquisite as the last.

After the third time, Kayla wasn't sure if she could move anymore, not even if someone set fire to the house. And then Alain surprised her again by gathering her into his arms. He didn't turn from her and just go to sleep, the way Brett had. The way she assumed most men did. Alain was actually *holding* her.

Oh, God, was he real? Or was she just dreaming?

"A penny for your thoughts," he said, noting the dazed expression on her face.

Busted. Kayla raised one shoulder in a shrug. "I'm just wondering why you're not being stalked."

He wasn't sure what he'd expected her to say, but it certainly wasn't that. "What?"

"Well," she began slowly, trying not to come off as a mindless idiot, "I'm assuming I'm not the first woman you've ever made love to. And given the insensitive lovers out there, someone like you would be quite a catch for any woman."

Did she have any idea how adorable she was? He smiled at her, his eyes softly caressing her face. "Maybe I was just inspired this time."

A content sigh escaped her before she could stop it. She knew he was probably just feeding her a line, but she pretended that he was telling her the truth.

So rather than go on talking, she nestled against him, taking comfort in the beat of his heart against her cheek. Indulging in a fantasy that this was going to go somewhere, beyond tonight.

And then, as her eyes began to drift shut, she suddenly found herself assaulted by a wave of lights, accompanied by a battalion of sounds as everything within her bedroom and the rooms beyond came to life. Every appliance, every light fixture, the TV, the radio, everything she'd turned on when the power had gone out, hoping to find a spark of electricity, came on at the same moment, generating a swirling tornado of light and noise.

Startled, she bolted upright. Alain was right beside her, as surprised as she was.

"And then there was light," he said, looking around. His gaze returned to Kayla, who was sitting up, nude to the waist. His smile grew sensual as he reached for her. "This time," he said to her, "I get to see what I'm doing."

But just as he leaned in to kiss her, the phone on the nightstand began to ring.

His face an inch away from hers, Alain's eyes widened as the sound registered. "The phone." He looked up at it. "Your phone's ringing."

She knew what he was thinking. Phone service had been restored along with the power. That meant he could call someone to come get him.

And take him from her.

She knew that was inevitable; she just hadn't thought it would happen tonight. A huge wave of disappointment washed over her.

"So it is." Resigned, Kayla turned away from him and reached for the phone. She brought the receiver to her ear. "Hello?"

"Kayla, where've you been? I've been calling your number for over a day and no one's been answering." The deep male voice on the other end of the line was loud enough for Alain to make out.

It was Jack Brown, one of the volunteers she occasionally worked with at the rescue center. She struggled to focus.

"We had a power failure here," she told him. They didn't socialize, so this had to be about dogs. "Is something wrong?"

"Yes, something's wrong," he told her, although his voice no longer sounded as upset as it had. "I have a couple of shepherds in the Riverside shelter that aren't going to live out the week unless someone comes to claim them."

It was a familiar story. She'd traveled up and down the length of Southern California and beyond, going to the city shelters and rescuing German shepherds marked for extermination. At times, it felt like a never-ending battle.

Nodding as Jack gave her a few more details, she

interrupted and asked for the address, just to be sure she had the right shelter. "All right, tell them I'm coming. I'll be there as soon as I can manage. Probably around noon tomorrow. Thanks for calling."

Business as usual, Kayla thought, hanging up. Then, picking up the phone, she shifted in the bed and offered it to Alain. She tried to sound cheerful as she said, "Your turn."

But he didn't take it from her. Instead, he asked, "Who was that? Someone needing a vet?"

She shook her head. "Someone needing an angel of mercy," she corrected. That was the way they saw themselves, the members of the rescue team. Angels of mercy for a constant stream of furry orphans. "Two German shepherds were located at a Riverside shelter—they're usually euthanized within two weeks after arriving at one of the city shelters. There are just too many stray and abandoned dogs out there to keep them all alive."

That was the excuse, but he could see how much the reality of it bothered her.

"And you're riding to the rescue?" He assumed that from her end of the conversation.

A self-deprecating smile played on her lips. "It's what I do."

Nodding, Alain glanced at his watch. It was a little after 10:00 p.m. Not late by his standards, but he knew that Philippe liked to get to bed early so he didn't drag the next day. His eldest brother had always been an early riser, unlike Georges. *And him.*

Making up his mind, Alain shook his head and gently pushed away the phone that Kayla was holding out to him.

"It'll keep until morning," he assured her. He watched as she struggled with the sheet she'd wrapped around her breasts, replacing the phone on the nightstand. When she turned back to him, he grinned at her. "Now, where were we?"

"Again?" she asked incredulously. The man was absolutely incredible, she thought.

"Unless you're too tired," he qualified.

His thoughtfulness touched her. Most men wouldn't have worried about whether she was as keen on another go-around as they were. But making love with him had taken on a new urgency for her. This would be the last time, she realized. Tomorrow, he would make his call to his brothers or a friend, and once they came for him, he would be out of her life within a matter of hours, if not less.

Granted, his car was in Mick's shop, but he could always send someone up for it. And even if he did return for the vehicle himself, there was no guarantee that he would stop by her place. Most likely he wouldn't.

They were from two different worlds. No one had to tell her that.

But she forced a smile to her lips as she slid down against the pillow and looked up at him. "Too tired?" she echoed. Her eyes softened. "Alain, I'm just getting warmed up."

"Good," he said, pulling her to him. "That makes two of us."

Chapter Nine

When morning with its bright, glittering sunshine crept into the bedroom, Alain found himself experiencing a strange reluctance to stir or even open his eyes.

His reluctance had nothing to do with the aches and pains still riding roughshod over him. They were purely physical, and he knew that once he started moving, they would work themselves out relatively soon.

No, his reluctance to acknowledge morning stemmed from the fact that once he did, he was going to have to resume his life. Placing a call to Philippe, which was the first thing on his agenda, would instantly connect him with that life, and this adventure would, in essence, end.

He'd be leaving.

Leaving a simpler way of life, one he'd thought would quickly drive him up a wall—but hadn't.

Leaving Kayla.

The long and short of it was, he didn't want to leave her. Not yet. Not when he'd only just begun to enjoy being around her.

The fact that he did was nothing new. He'd always enjoyed being with women, enjoyed the company of vibrant, independent females who knew what they were about.

But he'd learned never to require the company of any particular woman for long. Because, for one reason or another, they would leave. The nannies he grew attached to had always left, some sooner than others. Throughout his childhood and adolescence, his mother was always leaving. So Alain became very good at not needing them to remain. Eventually, he became the one who left first.

But his time with Kayla had been much too brief. Barely three days, and the first really didn't count, inasmuch as he really hadn't been himself.

Still, maybe it was better this way. Better because he had a feeling that, though it hadn't happened for more than a decade and a half, he could become attached. Attached to this woman with the laughing eyes, the killer smile and the heart as big as all outdoors. And he'd long since learned that attachments were only unions begging for severance. For disappointments. He knew this as well as he knew his own name. There was no reason to expect anything else, anything different.

Damn it, he needed to shake off this malaise. He needed to get on his way.

Alain forced himself to open his eyes, to take the first step that would set him on the path to the rest of his life.

He was alone except for the dog in a cast staring him in the face.

Winchester.

But not Kayla.

Absently, he petted the animal as he sat up. Opening his mouth to call out to her, Alain thought he heard noises coming from somewhere in the house. Pots being moved. A refrigerator being opened and closed.

Kayla.

A warmth spread over him. He fought a desire to get up and go looking for her. A desire to bring her back to bed and go through a reenactment of last night.

Damn it, what was wrong with him?

Annoyed with himself, Alain reached for the phone instead. First things first.

Picking up the receiver, he held it to his ear. It was

then that he realized he was holding his breath. Waiting to find out if the phone was actually still working? Or hoping that it wasn't?

The latter seemed foolish, but he really couldn't have said with any amount of certainty which direction his hopes were aimed.

This place had scrambled his brain.

Just as she did.

Maybe this town *was* like the fictional Brigadoon, seducing whoever came upon it into remaining, committing his soul to a timeless world where life was a great deal simpler.

But the world beyond Kayla's home was beckoning to Alain. His fingers punched in Philippe's phone number on the keypad before he could talk himself out of it. The phone on the other end rang only twice before someone picked up. And then he heard Philippe's deep voice say hello.

There'd been a time, whenever his older brother picked up the phone, that he would sound incredibly grumpy. Philippe didn't like being interrupted. The oldest of Lily Moreau's sons worked at home. He had made his fortune and his mark on the software world by withdrawing into his home office and wrestling with concepts that completely mystified the rest of the family. Because it took so much deep concentration, he hated having to focus on anything else while he was working. This included incoming calls, even from the companies that he was dealing with.

But J.D.—Janice—had changed all that, had completely remodeled Philippe's house and his world. These days, his brother was positively sunny and damn near unrecognizable.

So it was a remarkably cheery voice that said, "Zabelle here."

"Philippe."

"Alain!" The concern in his brother's voice was palatable. "Where *are* you?"

"Funny you should ask," Alain murmured. "I'm not in Bedford."

"I already know that," Philippe answered with a touch of impatience. "You haven't been home the last three nights."

Alain knew he could tell that simply by walking out his front door. They lived next door to one another, he and his brothers, in houses that, to the passing eye, formed what appeared to be a single sprawling mansion. In reality, there were three attractive homes made to look like one huge estate.

That had been Philippe's idea. He'd grown up caring for his brothers, and it was a habit he didn't seem to want to break. In truth, though neither Alain nor Georges admitted it aloud, they liked the arrangement, liked being close, yet able to maintain separate lives. Again, all Philippe's doing.

Taking a deep breath, Alain forged ahead. "I was in an accident."

The concern was immediate. "Are you all right?"

"Yes," he quickly assured him. "But that's more than I can say for my car."

He heard Philippe sigh. Material things had never been a priority with him. "All right, tell me what happened."

Alain knew that there was no way he was getting off the phone until he gave Philippe every single detail of the accident, what led up to it and what had transpired afterward. He summarized the events as quickly as he could, talking faster and faster. Trying to outrun the reluctance that was mushrooming through him.

And when he was through, he concluded, "So I need a ride."

It was obvious the request was nothing less than Philippe had expected. "I'll be there as soon as I can," he promised.

Why did that make Alain's heart sink a bit? "You don't have to leave immediately," he told him. "Wait for the traffic to die down."

His brother would have to drive through the snarl of L.A. traffic to get to him. Traffic that, at its peak, crawled rather than flowed—if that. Alain felt bad enough already about asking him to come get him. He didn't want him stuck in bumper-to-bumper congestion.

"I'm on my way," Philippe replied firmly.

"Right." Obviously, his mind was made up. "Thanks."

No sense in trying to talk his brother out of it. No one, Alain thought, letting the receiver fall back into the cradle, could tell Philippe what to do—with the possible exception of Janice, or Kelli, her pint-size daughter.

There'd been a lot of changes in the family of late. Philippe was getting married next month, and Georges wasn't going to be lagging far behind, now that he'd lost his heart to a woman with the improbable name of Vienna. And Alain wouldn't be surprised if Gordon, Janice's older brother, wasn't going to be making an announcement soon himself. Georges's cousin Electra had set her cap for the man, and both she and Gordon seemed exceedingly happy about the arrangement.

Alain's cousins, Remy, Vincent and Beau, were still very much ensconced in the bachelor life, so he wouldn't feel like the last holdout. But it wasn't exactly the same thing as having his brothers unattached, without the responsibilities of hearth and home, and all that entailed.

Funny, when he was a kid, he'd been convinced things would never change—except for the faces of their mother's "companions."

It was, he knew, a foolish fantasy, and yet he couldn't quite help the longing he felt....

"Coffee?"

The cheerful voice broke through his thoughts, scattering them like mist. Roused, Alain looked toward the doorway.

Kayla was standing there with a large mug in her hand, a faint curl of steam rising above it. The scent of coffee began to fill the room.

The scent of coffee and the light perfume she wore.

"Sounds great."

Alain shifted in the bed as she crossed to him. He was about to reach out for the mug when he realized he was still very much unclothed beneath the sheet spread haphazardly over him. The second the realization hit him, temptation sprinted through him.

"You know what sounds even better?" Accepting the mug, he placed it on the nightstand.

Her eyes were wide. "What?"

Alain curled his fingers around her wrist. Her warmth spread into him. "Guess."

"Breakfast?" she asked innocently. Or at least she tried to sound innocent. In actuality, her heart was racing like a yearling at its first major event.

She'd thought that she could pull this off, that she could sound blasé and sophisticated, like the women she assumed populated his world. She knew he was going to be leaving this morning, or at the very latest, this afternoon. She'd thought she'd made her peace with that. But obviously, she hadn't.

What was going on here? She had no desire to fall into any tender trap. No desire to get caught up again in all the briars and brambles that were part and parcel of being with someone. With caring about someone.

And yet here it was, uninvited. She didn't seem to have any say in the matter, any say in what she felt or didn't feel.

She didn't *want* to feel anything.

But she did.

All the worse for her, because he *was* going to be leaving, Kayla told herself. And she didn't want his last thoughts about her to be filled with pity.

"Not even close." Alain gently drew her down onto the bed. His eyes held hers. "That's not the appetite that's stirring."

"You called your brother." He'd made no effort to lower his voice, so she'd overheard his part of the conversation. *Because you were straining for the sound of his voice, idiot,* she upbraided herself. "Shouldn't you be getting ready? Or isn't he coming?" Oh, God, did that sound as hopeful as she feared it did?

"Oh, he's coming. The sun will stop rising before Philippe stops being dependable. But it'll take him more than two hours to get here." Alain found himself actually rooting for the traffic. How strange was that? "Maybe three."

"Two hours," Kayla echoed, the last bit of any resistance ebbing away. She'd turn off the eggs she was making, because part of her had hoped...

"Maybe three," he repeated softly, beginning to unbutton the blouse she was wearing. Sending hot tongues of desire radiating all through her. "And seeing as how I'm already 'dressed' for the occasion..."

He gently tugged the ends of her blouse out of her jeans. Leaning forward, he feathered a kiss along the side of her neck. Her eyes fluttered shut as she released the last of her grip on decorum.

Wild things began to happen within her. Wild, delicious things. She scarcely remembered helping him, scarcely remembered tearing off her clothes and slipping, sleek and naked, back into her bed.

For one last visit to paradise.

Kayla couldn't readily recall the last time she'd felt this awkward. As far back as she could remember, she had always felt comfortable in her own skin. Oh, there was that short period of time when she'd allowed herself to be sublimated into the kind of woman that Brett had wanted, a person he could order around. She'd allowed it to happen because she'd loved him, or told herself she did. But she'd quickly snapped out of it the second she'd come to her senses.

Other than that, she'd always been confident in any given situation, confident in her own abilities.

She felt at loose ends right now.

It had nothing to do with the tall, good-looking man standing in her living room. He had a kind smile, and she found herself liking him instantly. Alain's older brother radiated authority, but in a good way.

Philippe Zabelle had Patriarch written all over him, even though he didn't appear to be that much older than the brother he'd come to fetch.

He'd already thanked her twice for rescuing Alain. Not only that, but he'd looked genuinely interested when she'd shown him her "foster" dogs. Especially Ginger's puppies.

"I'd like to come back and adopted one of them when they're ready to leave their mother," he'd told her. Alain had looked at him quizzically, but he'd addressed his words to her. "My daughter would just love a puppy."

My daughter. Not "my fiancée's daughter," or "my stepdaughter," but "*my* daughter," even though, from what Alain had told her, the wedding was still more than a month away. He'd obviously taken the little girl to his heart. Yes, Kayla had found herself instantly liking this man.

The awkwardness stemmed from the fact that she found herself missing Alain even though he was still standing here.

What was she going to do about that?

Move on, she told herself firmly. Because life was going to do just that, move on. Whether or not she chose to come with it.

Alain noticed that Philippe seemed to be retreating, edging toward the front door. They had to get going.

"I'll wait for you outside," he told him, then nodded at Kayla. "Nice meeting you. And thank you again for taking care of Alain."

Before she could brush his thanks away again, Philippe closed the door behind him. Leaving the two of them to say goodbye.

Alain felt his breath catch in his throat, blocking the words. Why did she have to look so damn desirable again? It wasn't like he could just stay here, making love with her three times a day. He had a life to get back to. A rich, full, *busy* life.

The word *goodbye* refused to emerge.

"Um, look…" He pulled his checkbook out of his jacket pocket. "I'd like to pay you—for your help," he added quickly, when he saw her eyes widening in shock and something he couldn't fathom.

Kayla drew herself up, squaring her shoulders. Had he just insulted her? That was the last thing he wanted to do.

"I didn't do it for your money." She took a breath, as if trying to quell a flash of temper. "Just pass it on. Help someone else in trouble if you get the chance."

Her voice suddenly sounded distant, as if she was closing off from him. But he needed to do this. Whether it was his conscience or something else at play, he didn't know, but a small token of appreciation would make things better.

Wouldn't it?

"At least let me make a donation to your organization." She began to demur again, but he was already writing out a check for a generous amount. Tearing it off, he held it out to her. "You can fill in the correct name. I'm afraid I don't remember it."

She glanced at the amount. That couldn't be right. "You put in too many zeroes," she told him.

Alain looked at the check, then shook his head. "No, I didn't."

"That's for a thousand dollars." The most she'd ever gotten was a hundred. Most donations were in the tens and twenties.

"Yes, I know."

It was guilt money, she thought. Somehow, he was trying to soothe his conscience.

About what? The man didn't owe her anything. No promises had been exchanged. Just a good time.

She forced herself to smile. The money would go a long way toward the care and feeding of needy animals. God knew they could use it. It would certainly buy a lot of dog food. Besides her seven-plus, there were currently forty-five unadopted dogs living with a handful of volunteers, and that number fluctuated on a regular basis, usually growing rather than decreasing.

"All right, to help the dogs," she said, taking the check from him.

He found himself wanting to do more for her. And to postpone leaving for at least another minute or so. "Look, my mother knows a lot of people," Alain said suddenly. "Maybe, around the holidays, she could throw a fund-raiser, get some *real* money for your organization."

Kayla nodded, but she really didn't believe a word he was saying, and doubted that he did, either. It was like that old line, "we'll stay in touch," uttered at parting, by kids still in the throes of a summer romance. The intent was there, but it wouldn't happen. There'd be no fund-raiser, no Alain. This was it. He was leaving and she'd never see him again.

Still, she tried to look as if she believed him. "Sounds good," she murmured.

Before he could stop himself, Alain took her into his arms. Damn, but she felt good. As if she belonged there.

What the hell are you thinking? Just how hard did you hit this head of yours?

Taking a deep breath, he allowed himself one quick, fleeting kiss. Not a lingering one, but a fast brush of lips. And then he was letting her go, and the emptiness was seeping in.

"Thanks for everything."

His parting words hung in the air long after he shut the door and left.

Chapter Ten

"She seems like a nice woman."

The comment splintered the silence that had infiltrated the interior of his car. Philippe didn't know what to make of it. Ordinarily, he was the quiet one in the family.

Thinking back, he had never known a time when Alain *wasn't* talking. Which was why, when he'd announced at the tender age of ten that he intended to become a lawyer, it really seemed like the natural choice for him. Though Georges was no shrinking violet, of the three of them, it was Alain who truly had the gift of gab. He had always been as talkative, as outgoing, as their mother. Maybe even more so.

Which made his silence now almost eerily unnatural.

Alain took in a deep breath before answering. "Yes," he said quietly. "She is."

Something was definitely wrong here, Philippe thought. This just wasn't like Alain. They were on a two-lane road, making their way to the coast and Interstate 5. He spared his brother a glance, looking at the bandage on his forehead covering the gash that had been sewn up. Was there a concussion that had been overlooked?

"Maybe I should drive by Blair Memorial when we get back home, take you to the emergency room," Philippe suggested. He'd never been an obsessive worrier, but there was nothing wrong with being thorough.

Lost in his own thoughts, trying to extricate himself from a quagmire of emotions that threatened to pull him under, Alain frowned. Philippe's suggestion seemed to come out of the blue. "Why?"

"To get you checked out," he answered simply. "You don't sound like yourself." He thought of the uncustomary silence. "Hell, you don't 'sound' at all. I've never known you to be quiet. You even talk in your sleep—at least you did when you were a kid." The road straightened and he pressed down on the accelerator, speeding up in order to pass a truck.

"I'm all right," Alain told him, his voice flat. "I don't need to go to any hospital."

Philippe debated turning on the radio to ward off the quiet, but decided that it would only be a distraction. They had at least an hour before they would reach Orange County and more before they got home. They might as well have this out now.

"Convince me." It was a softly spoken order.

Alain bristled, surprised at how short his temper was. He didn't usually have one. "What do you mean, convince you? Why do I need to convince you?"

The answer to that was simple. "Because if you don't, I am taking you to the hospital." It didn't matter that his passenger was a full-grown adult and slightly taller than he was. Philippe had always been the patriarch and he didn't intend to relinquish the role anytime soon.

Alain dismissed his brother's words. "What I need is to get to work—" he looked down at what he was wearing "—and a change of clothes. I've been living in these since Friday...." He saw Philippe glance at him. And sniff to check if the air around him was ripe. "After Kayla washed them," he added.

Little pieces were being nudged into place in Philippe's head. "What did you wear while that was happening?" He asked, his tone innocent.

"A blanket."

Alain saw a hint of a smile curve the corner of his Philippe's mouth and knew exactly what he was thinking. That he and Kayla had gotten it on. After all, that was the reputation he had. He felt defensive, not for himself but for her.

What the hell was that all about?

"Don't give me that look. She was just being practical. I was soaking wet and unconscious. She was afraid I'd get pneumonia. She's the one who bandaged me up and stitched my head."

He couldn't read Philippe's expression. Surprise? Skepticism? A bit of both? "She's a doctor?" he asked.

Alain turned his head, presumably to look out the window, before he answered.

His voice was so low that Philippe couldn't hear what he said above the rumble of traffic. They'd just gotten on the freeway. "What?"

Alain didn't turn his head, and made no attempt to speak up as he repeated his answer.

If Philippe was frustrated, he didn't show it. He just inclined his head toward Alain and said, "One more time."

"A vet, a vet, a vet," he fairly shouted, this time turning toward his brother. Trying to rein in his temper, he glared at him. "All right?"

Philippe acted as if his answer had been tendered

in a voice several decibels lower. "Being a vet is fine. What's not fine is your attitude." And then a small spark of annoyance was evident. "What the hell's gotten into you?"

Alain crossed his arms, thinking that he was acting like a jackass, but unable to stop himself. "Nothing." He knew that he had to give Philippe some kind of an excuse for his lapse in temper, so he thought of work. "I just don't like losing time, that's all. I was supposed to be at Dunstan's brunch on Sunday to talk over strategy, and I needed to be in touch with Bobbie Jo Halliday over this weekend, as well." He still hadn't told the woman about the valet's favorable testimony. That, along with everything else, clearly had them winning their case.

Why didn't that make him happy? Winning always made him happy.

Philippe had heard about the case his little brother had landed. "Ah, right," he said evenly, "the trophy wife trying to stick it to her late husband's kids."

Alain knew how Philippe felt about the matter. It was Philippe who had tried to instill a sense of fair play in him and in Georges. But this was different. This was the real world and his career they were talking about. "The will is in her favor."

Philippe nodded, signaling to change lanes and get away from a tanker truck. He'd never liked driving alongside a possible death trap. "Doesn't make it right," he countered.

Funny, he could almost hear Kayla saying the same thing, Alain thought. The woman probably had more in common with his brother than she had with him....

Why was he even thinking about something like that? What did it matter what they did or didn't have in common? She was just someone he was probably never going to see again. Except, maybe, if the fund-raiser came into being.

Where the hell had this wave of sadness come from? Maybe Philippe was right, maybe he did need a checkup.

"The law's the law," Alain replied belatedly, suddenly realizing that his brother was waiting for a response.

"Maybe," Philippe allowed. "But 'justice' is a whole different concept." He spared Alain a quick look. It was suddenly very important to him that Alain understood what he was saying—and agree with him. "What if Mother were to marry that juvenile who's wrapping her around his finger?" He was referring to Kyle Autumn, her latest protégé. Kyle had hung around longer than any of the others—except for her three husbands—and that was beginning to really concern Philippe. "And he got her to leave all her money to him. I have got a feeling you wouldn't be talking about 'the law being the law' then."

Alain shook his head, dismissing the comparison. "Mother wouldn't do that."

"But if she did?" Philippe pressed, not wanting to drop the matter. "If Kyle turned her head and made her feel that if she didn't change her will, he'd think she didn't love him. So she changes it and conveniently dies, what then?"

Alain didn't like thinking about things like that, didn't like being pressed or pushed to the wall. His thoughts were jumbled enough as it was. "Look, I don't want to talk about the case right now."

"All right," Philippe said indulgently, "what do you want to talk about?" He wasn't a big believer in sharing his own thoughts, but that didn't apply to the rest of them.

"Nothing." It was meant as a final response, a letting down of the curtain to announce that the show was over.

Except that it wasn't.

"That is definitely not like you," Philippe stated. He was silent for a couple of minutes. But just when Alain thought he'd gotten a reprieve, Philippe spoke again. And it wasn't about something innocuous, like the weather or sports. "It's that vet, isn't it?"

Alain could feel his back going up. Why couldn't his brother just drop it? How many times had they been in the car when *Philippe* didn't speak?

"What are you talking about?"

Philippe didn't answer his question. "What happened up there during the power failure?"

Alain reined in his thoughts, refusing to think about any of it right now. But he knew Philippe wouldn't back off until he gave him something. "We lived like pioneers."

Philippe waited. "And?"

Alain waved his hand impatiently. "And then the power came back on."

Philippe slanted a knowing look at him. "Yours or the electric company's?"

"What are you getting at?"

"Only that I've known you your entire life, watched you Romeo your way through an ocean of women, flashing that sunny smile of yours, and staying pretty much unaffected."

Alain had no idea why his guard was up, but it was. "Your point?"

"My point," Philippe stated patiently, determined to get to the bottom of all this, "is that you don't seem like the carefree bachelor you always were. Did something happen between you and that lady vet while you were waiting for the power to come on?"

Alain's answer was immediate and firm. "No."

Philippe read between the lines. "You slept with her, didn't you?"

He began to deny it again, then reconsidered. There were times he thought that Philippe probably knew him better than he knew himself. So he merely shrugged his shoulders. "There wasn't a whole lot of sleeping going on."

Philippe had lost count of the women who'd floated through Alain's life. But his brother had never been like this. Philippe drew the only conclusion he could. "And she got to you, didn't she?"

"No," Alain insisted, annoyed that he wouldn't just didn't let the subject drop. "She didn't 'get' to me." Philippe gave him a knowing look, causing him to protest, "We only made love last night. A person can't 'get' to you over the space of a few hours."

Philippe knew better. Janice had gotten to him the first moment he laid eyes on her. It just took him awhile to stop fighting it. "If you say so."

Alain loved and respected his brother and could sincerely say he was grateful Philippe had been in his life to steer him straight those times when he'd almost run aground. But this time, he was dead wrong. Alain refused to believe anything else. "I say so."

Philippe merely smiled.

Rather than take a few days off to recuperate and deal with his aches and pains, Alain threw himself back into his work. But to his dismay, the zest he'd always had for his cases just didn't seem to be there anymore. It was as if he was seeing everything in a different light.

It wasn't about winning anymore, it was about doing the right thing, just as Philippe had said.

As Kayla would have said had she known what he was about.

Memories of Kayla, of those few simple days he'd spent housebound with her, would sneak up on him unannounced, ambushing him when he least expected it. Interfering with his thought processes. Alain did what he could to banish the images, to place her and everything about her in a neat little box and shove it aside, the way he'd always done with the women he slept with.

He tried to forget about it, about Kayla, going on dates with a few women. No matter how good they looked, how much they tried to please, they all failed to measure up.

Failed to have the same effect on him, on his pulse, that Kayla had had.

That fact alone left him in a progressively worsening mood. He didn't want her to have that kind of effect on him, because if she did, that gave her a power over him. He'd seen what caring deeply about someone could do to a person, and he refused to let that happen to him.

That both Philippe and Georges were in love and firmly on a path that would lead them to marriage didn't convince Alain that happy endings were actually possible.

But he missed Kayla.

How could you miss someone you'd known for less than four days? he silently demanded as he stared, unseeing, at the Halliday case file. What was wrong with him? He was acting like some lovesick middle-school adolescent. Even when he'd been that age, he hadn't behaved like one.

Alain sighed and turned his chair away from his desk to stare out the window at a sky pregnant with dark, ominous clouds. Rain was coming, a storm by the looks of it. Just like…

This had to stop.

He was building her up in his mind. Making her into something larger than life, into something she wasn't. What he needed, he told himself, was to see her again—and see that he'd gotten carried away. That he had turned her into some sort of goddess in his mind.

What he needed, he decided, was to have her here, on his home turf. That would be his wake-up call.

The promise he'd made to Kayla just before he'd left came back to him. He'd told her that he would hold a fund-raiser for her organization. He grinned to himself. A fund-raiser. She couldn't turn that down. She'd *have* to come down for it.

He felt something quicken in his stomach and did his best to ignore it as he turned his chair back around and reached for the phone.

* * *

"A fund-raiser?" Lily repeated.

She'd been in her studio, agonizing over her latest effort, when her youngest son knocked and asked for permission to come in. Because inspiration was eluding her, she'd set down her brush and beckoned him in. She studied him now, surprised by the request. None of her sons ever asked her for anything.

"And it has nothing to do with art?" she asked.

Maybe he'd made his case too quickly. Lily always needed time to digest things, to mull them over as if she were staring at pieces of a puzzle.

"Not this time. It would be for an animal rescue organization. Volunteers find abused and abandoned German shepherds, take care of them and then place them with people."

Lily nodded. She'd always liked dogs, although she preferred little ones she could carry around and cuddle when the mood hit her.

"Well, that sounds straightforward enough," she commented. She looked at him curiously. "Why would they need a fund-raiser?"

It had been a long time since Lily had needed money. Both her paintings and her last two husbands, especially Georges's father, had made her a very wealthy woman.

His mother had forgotten what it meant to do

without, Alain thought. "To pay for food and medical expenses. Some of these dogs are boarded out until someone comes to adopt them. And some require a great deal of medical attention."

She cocked her head, curious. "Don't they have vets who volunteer their time? I thought I read something about that once."

He was certain that Kayla gave a hundred-and-ten percent of herself, probably using money she made as a practicing vet to help care for the animals she took in. But there were still limits.

"Their time, yes, but the supplies they use cost money." He knew his mother worked best with examples, so he decided to tell her about Winchester. As he thought of the dog, he couldn't help but wonder if Kayla had placed him yet, or if she still had him. It'd been close to three weeks since Alain had seen the dog—and her.

Rousing himself, he said, "There's one dog who was shot—"

That got his mother's attention. "Shot?" Her violet eyes opened wide. "Why on earth would someone shoot a poor dog?"

Alain gave her the answer that Kayla had given him. "Target practice."

Lily covered her mouth with her hands, genuinely appalled. "How awful. That poor creature." Her eyes flashed. She had always been on the side of the downtrodden. "Whoever did that should be drawn and quartered."

"No argument," he agreed, and quickly brought the conversation back on track. "But about the fundraiser... Do you think you could use your considerable influence to get some of your friends to attend and donate toward the cause?"

She smiled at his choice of words. They both knew he was flattering her, but she enjoyed it nonetheless. "Darling, you pour enough liquor and I can get them to donate to anything." Standing on her toes, she took his face between her hands, affection shining in her eyes as she looked at him. "I could never say no to you," Lily told him.

Alain didn't quite remember it that way, but now wasn't the time to remind her of all the junkets she'd taken, leaving the three of them behind with paid strangers. All the times he'd called to her to stay. That was in the past and he was none the worse for it now.

So he smiled, covering her hands with his own. "I was counting on that."

She studied him for a moment. "This means a lot to you, doesn't it?"

Alain thought it best not to admit to that, not even to himself. He didn't answer directly. "I gave my word to someone."

He was too much like her for her to believe it was only that. Lily smiled. "You're being a lawyer, Alain.

Be my son." And then her expression turned serious. "I know that perhaps I don't have the right to ask that of you, considering I was never much of a mother."

He'd stopped blaming her a long time ago. As Philippe had pointed out, she was just being Lily. And they all loved her.

"Oh, I wouldn't—"

Lily pressed a forefinger to his lips. "Don't interrupt, dear," she chided. "I don't apologize very often. I do want you to know that I was the best mother I could be."

Alain kissed the top of her head. "You were fine, Mother. And we always had Philippe. Let's see…a software engineer, a doctor and a lawyer." They'd all chosen a productive career rather than growing up to be spoiled, rich blots on society. "I'd say the three of us turned out pretty well."

"Yes," she agreed with affection, "you did." She looked back at her canvas and felt a rush. It was time to paint. But first, she needed to put this to rest. "All right, when do you want this fund-raiser?"

He knew his mother was mercurial, and her attention span had a tendency to shift without warning. "As soon as possible."

"Then it'll be as soon as possible," she agreed with a laugh. "A week from Saturday suit you?"

He hadn't expected it to be *that* fast. Alain grinned at his mother. "Perfect."

She raised her head and patted her hair, a wicked smile curving her lips. "So they tell me."

"C'mon, Winchester, you have to eat," Kayla begged. The forlorn dog lay listlessly on the floor at one end of the sofa. He'd pulled down the small cushion earlier, and now had it between his paws, resting his muzzle on it. The choice had mystified her, since the dog was nothing if not well behaved. And then she remembered that Alain had laid his head on the cushion, using it as a pillow. Winchester was just looking for his scent.

Makes two of us, she thought.

The next moment, she roused herself. She must have been under some kind of spell. There was no other way to explain her actions. She had never, ever gone to bed with a man she'd known only a matter of days. That was tantamount to a one-night stand.

Well, wasn't that what you had? A one-night stand?

They'd only had that one night. Why was she making such a big deal out of it? He obviously hadn't. It had been more than three weeks and he hadn't called her, hadn't tried to get in touch with her in any way. He hadn't even phoned about his precious car—which was taking Mick longer than he'd anticipated to fix. He was waiting for a part to be flown in, meanwhile working on the vehicle on good faith.

Kayla placed a dish of food beside the dog, who merely turned his head away.

"That's beef stroganoff," she told Winchester, just in case his keen sense of smell had deserted him. "Your favorite, remember?" But as she tried to coax him to sample at least a little, the dog turned his head to the other side. He had been eating less and less, ever since Alain had left. "Look, I know how you feel, but starvation isn't the answer. Don't make me force-feed you, Winchester."

His only response was to sigh.

That made two of them.

Chapter Eleven

When Alain first placed the call to Kayla, to his annoyance, he experienced all the nervous anticipation of the town geek asking the town beauty to the prom. So when he got her answering machine instead of her, he found himself doubly frustrated.

Assuming she was out on call, he waited until the following morning to try again. And again. And still again. Each time, her phone rang ten times, then her recorded message came on, calmly asking for details and a phone number where the caller could be reached.

He didn't want to talk to a machine, even if it was

her voice on the recording. He wanted to talk to her, to hear Kayla say his name. To hear the surprise in her voice because he'd hunted down her phone number and made good on his promise to get back to her about the fund-raiser.

Where was she? Out on a call involving some sort of lengthy emergency with someone's beloved pet? Or was she out all night with another man? Lying in someone else's arms the way she'd lain in his?

He knew he had no right to be feeling what he was right now. After all, the woman couldn't be expected to sit by the fireplace, pining away for him.

It didn't change how he was feeling.

No strings, remember? The way you always want it, right?

He slammed his briefcase shut on the kitchen counter. The lid bounced a little before settling down again. If there were no strings, why the hell did he feel so damn tangled up inside? And why, when her answering machine came on after his fifth attempt to get her, did he feel something akin to molten lava bubbling up within him, ready to spill out on anyone and anything? She could just be out with a friend, not a man. Alain hadn't a shred of evidence to support the wild, half-formed thoughts in his head.

It was as if despite all his legal training, his sharp mind had somehow turned to pudding, of absolutely no use to him.

He picked up the receiver again, then with a curse, let it drop back down in the cradle. There was no point in hitting Redial: he'd only get the machine.

Disappointment infiltrated, leaving a larger imprint than he thought possible. He'd been anticipating giving Kayla the good news that he had gotten his mother on board about the fund-raiser, and that Lily was even now pulling it together. He wanted, he realized, to reappear in Kayla's life, galloping up on a white charger and being her knight in shining armor.

He wanted Kayla to be grateful to him. Hell, he wanted Kayla, pure and simple. Ordinarily, the impressions left by women who passed through his life faded rather swiftly. But this time, nothing had faded. If anything, it had increased. He vividly remembered every moment of their lovemaking.

Remembered and longed for more.

Maybe he was coming down with something, Alain thought. Even so, he picked up the receiver one more time. This time, when he got the recording, he left a message, doing his best not to sound as put out that she wasn't there as he felt.

Just as he started to speak, he heard the doorbell. He ignored it and left his message.

"Kayla, this is Alain Dulac. I've got an update on that fund-raiser I mentioned to you. Give me a call back when you get in."

Whoever was at his door was now knocking. Alain quickly rattled off his cell number into the phone, then hung up.

The knocking grew louder. He needed to get going or he'd be late for work. He was definitely *not* in the mood to deal with whoever was on the other side of his door. Probably some impatient fool who was going to offer to do his gardening for him at a cut rate.

Or worse, it could be someone out to save his immortal soul by trying to convert him to the only true religion. He knew what his soul needed right now, and it had nothing to do with converting.

Alain was feeling far less than friendly as he picked up his briefcase and crossed to the front door, ready to go out. Whoever was there had damn well picked the wrong morning to throw a sales pitch in his direction.

A few cryptic words intended to send the intruder on his way hovered on his lips as Alain swung open the front door. He stopped dead, the words aborted.

Kayla. And a dog.

She summoned all her energy into her smile, wondering why she felt so nervous. This was only an errand of mercy.

For who, you or the shepherd?

"You need a dog."

Stunned, Alain stared at Kayla, the sunlight filtering through her red hair, creating an aura about her as if she were Venus surfing on a half shell.

For a second, he was convinced that he was hallucinating. But she was still standing there after his heart had slammed twice against his chest. And hallucinations didn't come with overly eager German shepherds, reared up on their hind legs, madly licking his face while their tails doubled as metronomes set to triple-time.

Alain stumbled backward, whether from the force of the dog, or the surprise of having her materialize on his doorstep, he wasn't completely sure.

"Winchester, down," Kayla ordered, giving the leash one hard tug. The dog reluctantly obeyed, dropping down to all fours again, but never took his eyes off the object of his affection, and his tongue remained at the ready to deliver another prolonged, hearty greeting.

"You're here," Alain heard himself saying in disbelief.

"Yes, I am." She tugged on the dog's bright-red leash again as Winchester, newly separated from his cast, gave every indication that for once he was going to openly disobey one of her commands.

"How did you find me?" Alain asked in stunned surprise. He looked down at the barely harnessed ball of energy. "Did your dog track me?"

"Your address was on the check you gave me for

the organization," she reminded him. As a lawyer, this man was not the sharpest she'd ever encounter. Winchester began to tug again, and she wrapped the leash around her hand twice. "And he isn't my dog." She saw Alain raise his eyebrow quizzically, and decided that made him look sensuously adorable. "Apparently, he's yours."

"I don't understand."

Out of the corner of his eye, Alain saw his neighbor from across the street on her way to deposit garbage into one of the dark-green pails at the side of her house. She was blatantly watching them, as if she'd tuned into her own private soap opera. The woman had always taken a very active interest in both his and his brother Georges's life.

Alain stepped forward and placed his hand on the small of Kayla's back, gently urging her into his house. "Why don't you and Winchester come in?"

She was beginning to wonder if he was ever going to invite her inside. Why did he have to look so good? She was kind of hoping that the dire circumstances of their encounter had been what made him seem so attractive to her. But in the light of the Orange County sun, he looked even better than he had in Shelby.

With a nod, she stepped inside his house, careful to keep herself between Winchester and him until the dog calmed down a little and got accustomed to seeing Alain again.

That might go for both of you, she told herself wryly. "Thanks," she said aloud.

Alain closed the front door. He could almost hear the woman across the street sigh in exasperation. For the time being, he deposited his briefcase by the door. Looking down at the prancing German shepherd, he realized that the dog no longer had any bandages on his right front leg. "He's all healed."

Kayla nodded. "I took the cast off on Friday." She petted the animal, though Winchester hardly noticed. He was trying to get closer to Alain.

With a grin, Alain ran his hand over the dog's head. If he had any intention of stopping, Winchester wouldn't allow it. The dog kept repositioning his head under his hand each time it passed over his fur. Alain laughed and continued petting.

He looked back at Kayla, and something else occurred to him. There were no other dogs with her. "Where's the rest of your posse?"

"With friends." She'd divided up the animals among other volunteers in the group, the way she always did whenever her rescue missions took her out of town. This time, she wasn't all that certain she was going to be back before nightfall. "All except Winchester." She nodded at the dog. "He wanted to come see you."

Alain's mouth curved and the next words out of his mouth told her he was humoring her. The man didn't understand animals. But he would. Winchester would teach him.

"He told you that?"

"As a matter of fact—" she smiled down at the dog, then raised her eyes to Alain's face "—yes."

The second she looked at him, Alain felt something tighten within his gut. Damn, but he could get lost in those green eyes. He rallied as best he could. "I had no idea he was such a talented dog. How long has he been talking?"

She shook her head. "You don't need words to make yourself understood. He all but stopped eating when you left, and now he just mopes around all day." She could see the denial forming on Alain's lips, but she had more proof. "You left a handkerchief behind, and he carries it around with him wherever he goes." To prove her point, she dug into a pocket of her jeans and produced a very mangled scrap of cloth.

Alain looked at the handkerchief skeptically. "Is he sick?"

Winchester grabbed the handkerchief from her hand, then let it drop at Alain's feet, raising his head and looking at his adopted master soulfully. "Lovesick, maybe."

Suddenly eager and playful, Winchester began to run in circles around him. Only Kayla's sternly voiced command of "Winchester, sit. Stay," finally stopped the whirling dog. Alain looked at him, stunned. "And I'm the object of this lovesickness?"

She felt as if she was answering for both Winchester and herself. But he didn't need to know that. Didn't need to know that standing here, looking at him, was making her stomach knot. Nothing could come of this. They were from two different worlds, belonged to two different spheres.

And yet...

Kayla inclined her head. "Apparently."

Alain scratched behind the dog's ear and Winchester slipped into dog heaven, thumping his foot in rhythmic ecstasy. "But I'm not a dog."

"Maybe lovesick's the wrong word," she allowed. *It's more applicable to me than the shepherd.* "But he's been listless ever since you left. Doesn't play, doesn't really eat, hardly drinks. Here." She dug into her pocket and placed a few dog treats in his palm, closing his hand with both of hers. For a second, something leaped up inside of her. It stayed, levitating, as his eyes held hers. She reminded herself to breathe. "Offer him this."

"All right." Alain no sooner held out the treats than Winchester snapped his jaws over the two bone-shaped crackers—taking care not to injure the fingers that held them.

Alain instinctively pulled back his hand, then examined it. No marks, no pain. He looked down at the munching dog. Winchester devoured the treats like the hungry dog he actually was. "Wow."

Kayla folded her arms before her chest. "I rest my case."

Alain studied the dog for a moment. Granted, Winchester was a handsome animal, now that he looked at him, but that didn't alter anything. "So what are we going to do about this?"

She gazed at him, her conviction clear in her eyes. "I think that's pretty obvious. He's your dog." And she doubted if anything would readily change that. The German shepherd had adopted Alain, instinctively knowing he would have a good home with him.

But Alain was shaking his head. As if he believed he had a real say in the matter. "I don't have any room for a dog."

Kayla didn't answer immediately. Instead, she slowly looked around the space she was standing in. The living room had vaulted, cathedral ceilings that gave the impression of vast, open spaces. To the left was a staircase leading up to the second floor. Beyond the living room was a formal dining room. The kitchen, she imagined, was beyond that, and who knew how many rooms there were in total. When her gaze returned to his face, she didn't try hiding the fact that she thought he was dead wrong.

"You could fit my place in here twice over, with room to spare, and I have six dogs and nine puppies," she pointed out.

But Alain liked being free. That meant not having anyone depending on him for anything. He didn't bother trying to reconcile this with the fact that he'd always felt he would be there for either of his brothers—or his mother—should the need arise. Be that as it may, he wasn't ready to take on more.

He tried again, knowing, somehow, that this might be a losing battle. "I don't know the first thing about owning a dog."

There were books for that. And she could offer her services in the short run. The biggest hurdle had already been vaulted: the dog loved him.

She grinned, stooping down to Winchester's level and running her hands over his back affectionately.

"That's because you don't own the dog, the dog owns you. I can give you a few pointers if you like, and he is housebroken and trained. Besides that, I'd say that Winchester pretty much made up his mind about you. If I take him back with me, he just might waste away, pining after you."

"You really think that?"

There was no hesitation on her part. She was dead serious. "I really do."

Alain looked at her for a long moment. It was on the tip of his tongue to say he'd missed her. That he was actually indebted to Winchester because the dog had brought her back into his life, for however short a period. But he couldn't. Something—self-preservation?—kept the words from coming out.

The best he could do was fall back on an excuse. "I've been trying to get ahold of you."

She wanted to believe him, but if that was the case, if he had been trying to get her, what had kept him from succeeding? "Oh?"

He shrugged, suddenly feeling awkward. He *never* felt awkward. What was she doing to him? "I guess you were on your way here."

"You called this morning?" When he nodded, she was more than willing to believe him, even as she told herself that the man was a smooth talker and was probably only saying what he thought she wanted to hear.

And she did; she wanted to hear that so badly. Wanted to hear that he missed her. That he had felt at loose ends, the way she had ever since he'd left.

"Why?" she asked, holding her breath, telling herself that she was an idiot—but she just couldn't make herself run for cover. Not yet.

"That fund-raiser I mentioned." Was it his imagination, or did she look a tad disappointed? He'd thought for sure this was the best way to get on her good side. Alain forged on. "My mother thinks it's a great idea."

Try as she might, Kayla couldn't quite picture the very flamboyant Lily Moreau heading up a fund-raiser for abused, abandoned German shepherds. But if the woman was actually willing, who was she to question that? Heaven knew they could use the money. Kayla's own bank account was swiftly dwindling because the animals needed so much. So many who came to her attention were sick, hurt or both.

She nodded. "That's great. Any idea when it might be?"

"Saturday night."

The man was nothing if not full of surprises. She couldn't have possibly heard him correctly. "*This* Saturday night?"

"Yes." Alain gauged her tone. There was a note of hesitation in her voice. "You have plans."

"No, nothing out of the ordinary," she qualified quickly, not wanting him to know that she spent the most social night of the week at home, grooming her dogs.

If the truth be known, she hadn't gone out with a man, much less to bed with one the way she had with him, since she had left Brett. She had no time to invest in a relationship, only to be disappointed. Her dogs gave her all the affection she needed.

Or had, until Alain set her bed on fire.

She squared her shoulders like a warrior. "But I

would have appreciated a little bit of a warning ahead of time."

"I did try calling you this morning," he reminded her. His eyes narrowed just a touch as he added, "And last night."

She hadn't gotten in until almost midnight. When she'd walked through the door, the dogs had surrounded her. All except Winchester. That was when she'd more or less made up her mind to bring him with her on her run down to the shelter in Anaheim. "Last night Jake Walton had a sick cow."

He supposed that made sense. Still, the type of animal surprised him. "You treat cows?"

"I'm a vet," she reminded him.

"Sorry, I thought you just worked on dogs." Damn, that sounded lame. *He* sounded lame. Where was all that charm that came so easily to him? Where was that magnetism that he'd been told all but radiated from him? Why did he feel like some awkward schoolboy because the woman who'd kept popping up in his head when he'd least expected it had done the same on his doorstep?

Kayla supposed, if she lived in a city, she would have narrowed her field. But she was the only vet for miles, and that broadened her playing field. "Dogs are my specialty, but I pretty much treat any animal that needs me."

"And lawyers," he interjected.

She had no fondness for lawyers. Brett had been a lawyer. "I wasn't treating a lawyer, I was treating an injury."

Winchester had turned his attention to the briefcase on the floor. Rescuing it, Alain remembered what he'd been doing when he opened the door. Leaving.

"I've got to get to work, but why don't you make yourself at home? I should be able to be back before six." He would make sure of that. "We could—"

Kayla stopped him before he continued and got completely entangled in the wrong idea. She didn't want him thinking that she'd used Winchester as an excuse to see him. That would be putting all the cards in Alain's hand.

"This isn't exactly a social call," she told him.

The way she said it had him pulling up short. "Oh?"

"I had to come down to see about a German shepherd they're holding at the Anaheim shelter. She's scheduled for termination—" God, she hated the way that word tasted in her mouth "—by the end of the week. Since I was going to be down here anyway, and it seemed like you were the cure for what ailed him, I thought I'd drop off Winchester with you first."

This time, Alain put his briefcase down on the side table. "So you really are serious about giving him to me?"

"What made you think I was kidding?" She didn't

wait for an answer. "I really don't think you have a choice in the matter."

He supposed that having a pet around wouldn't be so bad. It would give him an excuse to see her after the fund-raiser. He grinned at her. "You always come on so forcefully?"

She'd never had to bully anyone into taking one of the dogs. There were plenty of people who loved animals. She supposed she *was* coming on a little strong here, but only because she really did think that Winchester would begin to waste away if he was separated from Alain.

Kayla played along. "It works better than saying 'pretty please with a cherry on top.'"

"Oh, I don't know." He drew a little closer to her. "Maybe you could try it."

She was about to tell him he was crazy, but then she shrugged, and pursed her lips to form the first word.

She never got the opportunity to say it out loud.

When her lips puckered, Alain swept her up in his arms and kissed her. Hard. The way he'd been wanting to all these weeks.

He felt her surprise and then her surrender. And then he felt her kissing him back. Just as hard as he was kissing her. The little moan that escaped sent shivers up and down his spine. And a desire for more.

Her head was spinning again. Just the way it had the first time he'd kissed her at her house. That night in Shelby hadn't been a fluke. He really did make her feel as if she was intoxicated.

Kayla wrapped her arms around his neck and sank into the kiss, drowning in it.

Her pulse hammered wildly when she finally drew her head back to look at him. It took her a second to catch her breath. "I was wondering when you were going to get around to that."

He held her close for a moment, enjoying the way the rhythm of her heart matched his. "Didn't want to grab you the second you turned up on my doorstep. Well, I did," he allowed, "but I didn't want to frighten you away." It was bad enough that one of them was scared beyond words—because he'd never felt an impact like this before and he was afraid it was going to undo him completely if he wasn't careful.

"I think if I ran," she told him, "Winchester would fetch me back."

He grinned. "Well, that seals the deal for me. How can I refuse a dog that can fetch women?"

"Woman," she emphasized. "Not women."

"Even better." He leaned over, about to kiss her again. She put her hands up on his chest, looking a little hesitant.

"I really have to get going." But even as she said it, she made no effort to draw farther away.

"Yeah, me, too." Still holding her to him, Alain glanced at his watch over her head.

Her body was heating at an alarming rate. She needed to leave, but her feet wouldn't obey. "What are you thinking?"

He wrapped his arm back around her again. "That I could call in late."

"But I can't." She needed to remember that she was a responsible person, not some neo-hippie who could gratify her whims at will and damn the consequences. "The shelter is expecting me, and I hear the traffic on the way is awful."

"Traffic *is* awful," he agreed. "It gets better by ten. You could leave then."

"Ten." She grasped his wrist and looked at his watch. "That's two hours away."

"Yes." His smile was nearly blinding. "I know."

Her eyes were wicked as she looked up at his face. "What'll we do until then?"

"We could show Winchester his new backyard and then…" His voice trailed off.

"Then?"

"Then," he repeated.

Abandoning words, he showed her. He pressed a kiss to the side of her neck. When he heard her draw in her breath, the sound excited him to the point that he wanted to take her right there, on his living-room floor. Take her the way he'd fantasized about over and over again.

He began to unzip her jacket. Her breath came more

heavily. With effort, she put her hands on his to stop him. "Don't you have to call your office first?"

He nodded, taking out his cell phone. He pressed one of the preprogrammed numbers, and when he got the machine on the other end, left a message that he was going to be delayed that morning.

Kayla was doing the same on her cell phone, leaving word at the shelter that she was stuck in traffic, but would be there by around ten or so.

The second she closed the lid, terminating the call, she found herself being caught up in his arms.

The kiss that followed rocked her to her toes, which were no longer touching the floor.

Chapter Twelve

The delicious euphoria began to dissipate, quietly tiptoeing into the navy-blues and whites of Alain's coolly decorated bedroom. Unwilling to release her grasp on the joy that had been feeding her very soul, Kayla struggled to hold on to the feeling a little longer. But reality being what it was, the euphoria was even now slipping through her fingers.

With a reluctant sigh, she turned toward Alain in the rumpled bed. Her heart insisted on lighting up again, and she grinned. "You know, we have to stop meeting like this."

He laughed softly, drawing her into his arms. He

liked holding her, just holding her and having her close like this.

Definitely not business as usual, he thought, and that did worry him. But for now, he wasn't going to think about it, wasn't going to think that he was letting himself get in too deep too fast. He was just going to enjoy the surge that making love with her created within him.

He shifted his head slightly and the bright-blue numbers on his digital alarm clock all but jumped up at him. How had it gotten that late so quickly? He should have been on the road long before now.

"I hate to love and run," he told her. Then, because temptation reared its head, he allowed himself one more kiss. It was quick but potent, and pregnant with promise of things to come.

And, oh, it was such an argument for staying right where he was.

"I *really* hate to love and run," he told her with feeling, "but a client's coming in and I've got to be there or my head is going to be served on a platter." Alex Dunstan, senior partner and a friend of his late father, was counting on him to be there this morning—or what was left of it. And Bobbie Jo Halliday absolutely refused to deal with any of the other members of the firm. She'd confided in him that she found them all inflexible. Alain wasn't sure if she meant emotionally or physically.

Kayla nodded. "The trophy wife with the newly changed will." There'd been a lot on the Internet and on the news about the woman lately. None of it overly flattering, except for the photos. The woman was built like a proverbial Greek goddess.

Alain looked at her in surprise. "You were listening."

That was a first, he thought. If he did happen to "talk shop" around any of the women he went out with, it always seemed to breeze in one ear and sail right out the other. Not that he had an overwhelming desire to bring his work out of the office with him, but being a lawyer was part of who and what he was. Then again, it had never mattered to him that none of his dates cared about that, because he'd always kept things nice and loose.

So why did he feel so pleased that Kayla had paid attention? That she took an interest in his work? He wasn't making any sense.

Kayla looked surprised that he was surprised. "Why wouldn't I be listening? You were talking."

He wasn't going to think about this. "No reason," he said quickly, then pressed a kiss to her bare shoulder, which suddenly looked incredibly sensual to him.

Warm tongues of desire began to radiate out from where his lips touched her skin.

"Stop right there," she ordered, moving her hand to block his mouth. When he raised his eyes, looking at her quizzically, she said, "You trail those lips along my collarbone and neither one of us is going to get to where we're supposed to be going, not for a long, long time."

His eyes swept over her body and she saw hunger flicker in them.

Right now, the only place he wanted to go was where he'd just been. "That might be a matter of opinion," he told her.

Her own longing threatened to get the better of her, but she had a dog to rescue. And Alain had a bimbo to counsel.

"Don't make me push you out of bed," she warned.

Keeping the sheet discreetly wrapped around her, Kayla bent over the side of the bed to retrieve her clothing. Garments were haphazardly strewn on both sides, his on one, hers on the other. Luckily, hers were where she could reach them.

Rather than risk getting up and suffering what could be the delicious consequences of appearing utterly nude in front of him, Kayla pulled her clothes under the sheet and began wiggling into them.

When he realized what she was doing, Alain laughed. "You know, in some countries, that would be considered a very enticing prenuptial dance."

Having successfully pulled on her underwear and bra, Kayla went to work pulling her jeans up her legs, one eyebrow raised in amusement. "But not in this one."

Rather than follow suit, Alain rose from the bed. Looking at him, Kayla felt the insides of her mouth transform into sun-dried cotton. He was as gloriously naked as the day he was born, and far better endowed.

She couldn't draw her eyes away.

Aware that she was watching, Alain shrugged nonchalantly. "It's faster this way."

"I doubt it."

If they'd both started to get dressed that way, naked and facing one another, Kayla was willing to bet they wouldn't have gotten very far. Even now, she found breathing evenly a challenge.

Kicking the sheet aside, she rose. As she did so, she pushed her arms through the sleeves of her shirt, then quickly buttoned it up.

She felt his eyes skim over her body, and felt naked all over again.

"Do you want a key so you can come back when you're finished rescuing that dog?" he asked in a husky voice.

She couldn't help wondering how many keys to his house were floating around out there, and how many other women he'd offered them to.

Don't ruin it. You know it's not going to last, but don't hurry it along. Don't examine things too closely, she warned herself.

Glancing in the mirror over the bureau, she took a deep breath as she ran her hand through her hair in lieu of a comb. Kayla did her best to sound nonchalant. "I'm not coming back."

She saw the confusion in his face reflected in the mirror. "But the fund-raiser—"

Kayla's eyes met his in the glass. "Isn't, according to you, until Saturday. I can't stay here until then."

He didn't see what the problem was. Alain found himself rather liking the idea, since there was a ready excuse in place: she'd be only there until the fund-raiser. They'd have a few nights to enjoy each other without the threat of it being more serious.

"Why not?" he pressed. "You shared your place with me."

"There was a power outage at the time." Kayla stepped into her shoes. "And," she reminded him, "you were stranded."

He leaned over her, his engaging grin making her stomach whirl counterclockwise. "I could have a friend drive into the power grid for me," he offered. "And there's a utility pole not too far from here. I could try merging your truck with it." His expression was the soul of innocence.

It was hard not to laugh. Harder not to fall into his arms. With effort, she managed to remain steadfast. "I'll pass, thanks."

She looked so serious, he realized he wasn't sure exactly what it was she was turning down. The tongue-in-cheek offer, him, or everything.

"You don't want the fund-raiser?"

"Yes, yes I do." *For more reasons than one.* But she couldn't stay here until then. "How could I turn down something so generous? I'll be back on Saturday for it. Early," she promised. "But right now, I have a dog to pick up and take back with me." She already had foster parents waiting to take in the neglected animal.

Fully dressed, Alain looked down at Winchester. The dog had stationed himself by the doorway, as if guarding who came and who went. He'd been there for the last hour. "What about Winchester?"

She didn't quite follow. Kayla glanced over her shoulder at the dog. Winchester had eyes only for Alain. "What about him?"

"Are you taking him with you?"

She thought they'd been over this. "No, I already said he was yours."

"It's not that I don't want him," he argued, "but I don't have anything that a dog needs." He had no dog food, no dish for the animal, nothing.

Kayla begged to differ. She'd seen the way Alain had interacted with Winchester at her place.

"You have love. The rest can be bought at a pet store. And," she added, feeling that she was sealing the deal, "I brought some things with me in the truck. A bowl, his food, some of his toys. And a simple new-owners instruction booklet."

The last item caught his attention. And made him feel a wee bit better about the situation. "They have things like that?" he asked incredulously.

"Probably." However, this particular one wasn't anything he'd find in a bookstore. "I just wrote down answers to a few of the basic questions you might have." She smiled. She intended to make this as easy as possible for Alain—and Winchester. "I figured you might need help, and this'll make you feel better."

"I'd *really* feel better if you stayed," Alain declared.

So would she, Kayla thought. But for a completely different reason. Which was why she needed to go.

She forced a smile to her lips. "You'll be fine."

He looked doubtfully at the dog, then at some of his more expensive pieces of furniture. The house definitely wasn't doggy-proof.

"But I'm going to be gone for the next eight hours," he protested.

She assumed he was gone that amount of time five days a week. "And this is different from any other day how?"

That was his point exactly. "It isn't. It's not fair to a dog to be alone all the time."

Half the people who had pets were gone the bulk of the day. "It won't be all the time. And he'll adapt to your routine. You just have to pet him and show him that he's appreciated."

He wasn't going to talk her out of giving him the dog, he thought. And he supposed he was warming to the idea. Committing to a pet wasn't the same thing as committing to a woman. The dog wouldn't suddenly pack up and leave on a whim or after an argument, unwilling to work things out. A dog represented loyalty and unconditional love.

But Alain couldn't just surrender. Not all at once. "Got an answer for everything, don't you?"

"Pretty much," she agreed, without a trace of smugness or vanity. She paused to pet Winchester. "We can put him out in the yard for now."

Alain looked down at the German shepherd. He supposed it would go well, but for now, it suited his purposes to play the uncertain new owner.

"Maybe you should come back when you're finished at the shelter." His voice was soft, coaxing. "For Winchester's sake."

She saw right through him. And she had to admit it amused her. "I'm sure Winchester will be just fine." She patted the dog's head. "Won't you, boy?" In response, Winchester wagged his tail enthusiastically. "See?"

"That's just a reaction to being petted," Alain protested. He followed her as she went down the stairs. Winchester wriggled past them, then bounded down the rest of the steps energetically. Reaching the bottom, he turned and looked back, waiting for them to join him.

Kayla turned around to look at Alain when she reached the landing. "Winchester understands what you tell him, and some things you haven't even said out loud."

Alain didn't bother hiding the skeptical look on his face. His expression all but said, *Yeah, sure.* "You're giving me a mind-reading dog?"

He'd learn, she thought. "Make fun if you like, but dogs are very intuitive, and German shepherds are the smartest of the lot."

Alain nodded, seeming to take in what she was saying, but she wasn't fooled. He didn't easily give up his convictions.

"Fine. Then maybe in between doing long division in his head, he'll come up with a plan to make you stay."

She paused to brush her lips against his. When all else failed, she could always fall back on her tried-and-true excuse. "Can't leave my dogs for that long."

He thought he'd found an inconsistency. "You said they were with other people."

"They are." Kayla picked up her purse from where she'd dropped it by the front door, and slung it over her shoulder. "But all of those people have German shepherds of their own. I can't ask them to be overwhelmed indefinitely."

When she'd first told him about what she did, he'd thought of it as a hobby, or a limited one-woman crusade. Now it sounded like some monumental undertaking, the logistics of which could rival the blueprints for the undertaking of D-day. "Just how many of these dogs are out there?"

Kayla only needed a second to do the tally in her head. "Currently, we have forty-nine that need permanent homes, although the number fluctuates daily."

"And until then, until someone adopts these homeless dogs permanently, you and your friends are caring for them?"

She grinned as she patted his cheek. "Now you're catching on."

He caught her hand, pressing it against his cheek a moment longer before he released it. "So why go out of your way to pick up another one?"

Kayla looked at him for a long moment, trying to gauge if he was serious. If it was the lawyer or the man asking the question, and if the latter, whether she was wrong about him.

"The dog is going to be put to sleep by the end of the week," she reminded him quietly. "How can I not?"

Alain didn't have an answer for that, or even a

comment. She realized that she'd wanted him to agree with her without hesitation. While he hadn't done that, at least he hadn't said anything to try to talk her out of it. She supposed that was something. A baby step in the right direction.

"I'll be here before four on Saturday," she promised him, opening the door. "Be good," she told Winchester.

And then she was gone.

"You *have* to help me, Hannah."

On her knees, Hannah Martingale Peters looked up from the display she was trying to rearrange, recognizing the voice before she saw Kayla approaching her.

Because of its small size, Shelby was one of the few holdouts when it came to chain stores. Martingale's had been opened by Hannah's great-grandfather, and everyone in her family had worked here at one time or another. Each generation had improved or expanded the store, leaving its mark.

While still only a single story, the building was sprawling, and the store offered a little bit of everything, the way a five-and-dime once might have.

Leaning a hand on the counter to help her gain her legs, Hannah softly cursed the arthritis that kept her from leaping to her feet the way she had once been able to.

She anticipated what was on the vet's mind. "Honey, Ralph and I have as many dogs now as we can handle. I'd like to help you out, but what with Jonas and Corky and—"

Kayla was quick to stop the outpouring of words. Hannah, a big-hearted woman loved by all, had the ability to go on and on about nothing for hours.

"No, it's not about the dogs. At least, not directly," she qualified. She saw interest pique in Hannah's blue eyes. "I have to attend a fund-raiser—"

Her mouth dropped open. "A fund-raiser? My, my, that is impressive."

Kayla knew the woman wanted details, and she was more than willing to give them—but only after her problem had been tackled and put to rest.

"I need a drop-dead-gorgeous dress to wear." She'd already gone through the ones on the racks and found nothing that suited her purpose.

Hannah gave her a tolerant look. "Well, darling, we don't stock dresses that might kill people. Have you checked out our newest collection? There are a few very pretty ones straight from L.A." A tall woman, Hannah eyed the town vet, thinking her a tiny thing that needed fattening. That was what happened when you had no family to look after you, she mused. "I think one of them might suit you just fine."

Kayla shook her head. "I've already looked,

Hannah." She caught her lower lip between her teeth, hoping against hope. Time was getting short. "Is there anything in the storeroom that you haven't put out yet?"

Hannah began to shake her head and then stopped, suddenly remembering what had accidentally arrived in the last shipment. The order had been a mistake.

"Well, there was one. I told Ralph to send it back. Nobody here has any need for a dress that sparkles." She laughed, recalling her own reaction to the slinky gown. "Can you just see it at a barbecue, or the fall fair? The hem would get all dirty—"

"Can I see it?" Kayla asked, hoping that for once, the woman wasn't exaggerating.

Hannah lifted one wide shoulder and let it drop. "If it's still here. Like I said, I told Ralph to send it back. Ordinarily, the man never does what I ask him to, but probably, just this one time—"

Kayla couldn't wait through Hannah's diatribe about the failings of her husband of thirty years. "Can you check?"

"Well, of course I can." She paused to straighten a sign, then looked at Kayla again. "You mean now?"

She nodded vigorously. "Please."

Rather than go, Hannah peered at her, squinting through her glasses. "I don't think I've ever seen you this excited about a dress before." With a heavy sigh, she abandoned the display and waddled toward the rear of the store.

No, she'd never been excited about a dress before, Kayla thought, but that was because she'd never had a man to impress. It had suddenly occurred to her, on the drive back to Shelby with the newest rescued German shepherd riding in the back, that a lot of women Alain had gone out with might be attending this fund-raiser. The last thing Kayla wanted was to look like a hayseed next to them. And she would if she wore any of the dresses in her closet. They were functional, not fancy.

Kayla raised her voice and called out, "Find it?"

"Still looking," Hannah responded.

She mentally crossed her fingers. She wondered if she'd have time—should Ralph have proved to be dependable this one time—to drive up to Santa Barbara for the sole purpose of buying a dress that threatened to melt the eyes of the beholder.

Probably not.

She said a small prayer that Ralph had not deviated from his normal slothful pattern.

Chapter Thirteen

For the umpteenth time, Alain pushed back the sleeve of his jacket and looked at his watch. As if staring at it could somehow make the small hour hand move backward of its own accord.

She was supposed to be here by now.

He distinctly remembered Kayla telling him that she would be here on Saturday at four o'clock. *Promising* to be here at four. Well, it wasn't four anymore. Or five, or six. It was ten after six. The fund-raiser was scheduled to begin at eight o'clock sharp, at his mother's house. The printed invitations said so.

To his amazement, Lily had moved at incredible

speed, contacting people and verbally twisting arms as she called in favors in that deep, honeyed-whiskey voice of hers.

He knew she wasn't doing it for an organization she'd never heard of; she was going to all this trouble for him.

Now, for some reason, Lily felt the need to try to make up for lost time. To make it up to all of them. She was bent on living life to the fullest, not as the toast of the art community, or the most celebrated hostess on four continents, but as a loving, doting mother.

She'd already thrown Philippe and Janice an embarrassingly ostentatious engagement party, and was just waiting for Georges to make a formal announcement—or even a whispered one—to do the same for him and Vienna. Lily had even taken on, rather enthusiastically, the role of Kelli's grandmother. Although everyone knew that to call her that to her face meant being the recipient of a world of hurt, where medieval tools of torture were involved.

But even though she'd seemingly undertaken this new role with gusto, Alain knew his mother well enough to know she would be far from pleased if Kayla didn't show up at the gala.

The legendary Lily Moreau did not suffer being embarrassed.

Why wouldn't Kayla show? he silently demanded,

beginning to pace about the living room. It didn't make any sense. She seemed so devoted to those dogs. The organization stood to make a lot of money. She wouldn't turn her back on that.

Pivoting on his heel to retrace his steps, Alain almost tripped over Winchester, who had become in only a few days his ever-present shadow.

"You know her, Winchester. Why isn't she here? If she was running late for some reason, why wouldn't she call to tell me?"

And why, he wondered silently, was he so wound up about a woman he hardly knew? Why was he all but dancing attendance this way? Why was he worrying?

He'd never done anything like this before, never gone so far out of his way to try to please a woman. Hell, pleasing women came easily to him, but that usually involved dinner, some form of entertainment and then a few hours of complete, pure physical pleasure. And that was it. Nothing more.

But this was different. *Felt* different.

This felt like involvement.

And with involvement came problems. A whole slew of them.

Alain didn't want to go that route, didn't want to feel the kind of pain he knew his mother had felt.

Damn it, what had he been thinking, asking her to do this? What was wrong with him? If it was Kayla's intention to—

His train of thought abruptly derailed. Winchester was suddenly alert, his head turned toward the front of the house. Every bone in his body appeared to stiffen in complete concentration.

"You hear something?"

Before the question was out of his mouth, Alain heard the doorbell ring.

He crossed to the door in record time.

As he pulled it open, Winchester suddenly nudged him out of the way. The next moment, the dog was prancing excitedly on his hind legs, his front paws on Kayla's torso, welcoming her the only way he knew how.

Alain could only stare. "You're all right."

"Which is more than I can say for this freeway system of yours," Kayla exclaimed. Her eyes blazed as she declared, "There are way too many people stuffed in down here."

She was obviously struggling to subdue an enormous case of road rage. She'd been stuck in traffic for an unforgivable amount of time, and cut off three times.

His relief at seeing her gave way to amusement. She looked adorable with smoke coming out of her ears.

"I'll see what I can do about sending them to another county." Abandoning the banter, he closed the front door and then physically moved Winchester out of the way. "My turn," he told the animal, pulling Kayla into his arms.

"You don't want to hug an uptight woman," she warned him.

There wasn't anything he wanted to do more. "Yes, I do," he retorted, tightening his arms around her just a bit. "I want to kiss one, too."

Oh, no, she wasn't about to let him lead her astray. She'd moved heaven and earth to find the right gown to wear to this thing, and she wasn't going to get sidetracked into not wearing it. "I've got to get dressed."

"We'll make up for lost time," he promised her, kissing the side of her throat. "I'll help you, I swear."

She was still struggling, but not nearly as much. "Yeah, right. That's like asking a coyote to watch the sheep."

"They've got a very strong union, I hear. The coyotes."

Whatever Kayla was going to say in protest was muffled as his lips came down on hers.

The frustration she'd brought into the room with her died a swift, painless death, swept away by the surge of feelings that erupted the instant their kiss began to flower.

On the long trip down from Shelby, she had done her best to talk herself out of feeling anything for Alain. She'd even listed all the reasons why nothing could come of her seeing him. Over and over, she told herself that she was investing in something that had no future. Heaven knew she didn't need to feel the pain of heartache, didn't need to once more court abandonment.

And abandonment would surely come. He was a playboy, emphasis on the word *play*. Granted, she didn't exactly have one foot in the grave, and there was still time to enjoy the lighter side of life before she settled down. But the truth was, she just wasn't built that way. She didn't know how to dally, how to have an interlude and just walk away. She didn't have sex, she made love. There was a huge difference. Her heart, despite all her internal lectures, was bent on settling down. On nesting.

And the more she was with Alain, the more she wanted to be with him.

The more she wanted the impossible.

Kayla realized that she was digging her fingers into his arms. Damn him, he was turning not just her knees into liquid, but her whole body, as well. Any second now, she was going down for the third time.

With effort, Kayla placed her hands against his chest and pushed. Or tried to. Her strength seemed to have deserted her. She'd never felt so feeble in her life.

She all but sucked in air the moment she pulled her head back. "Have you registered that mouth of yours yet?" she quipped. "It really is lethal."

Her stomach was fluttering like a flag in a hot Santa Ana wind.

"I never had complaints before," he told her.

"I bet you haven't."

And there it was in a nutshell. He'd kissed a legion of uncomplaining women. He was first and last a playboy. And right now, he was playing in Kayla's yard. But not for long.

As if it was going to hurt any less when he returned to his life, Kayla silently scoffed. She was already a goner and she knew it.

Well, if she was a goner, she might as well just enjoy the time she had, however short that might turn out to be.

Willing her pulse to stop scrambling, she said, "My dress for the fund-raiser is in the trunk. Where can I change?"

The look in his eyes was nothing if not wicked. "Right here would be nice."

The traffic had made her late, despite the fact that she had left early. There wasn't much time for her to turn into a butterfly. "Seriously."

"Seriously," Alain echoed, doing his best to keep a straight face.

They both knew what would happen if she took him up on that. "I change in here and odds are we won't make the fund-raiser on time."

All his earlier concerns had burned to a crisp the

second he'd kissed her. All he wanted now was to make love with her. "My mother'll understand. She's a romantic at heart."

I'll bet. For an intelligent man, he could be almost sweetly simple. "With everyone but her sons," Kayla told him.

"What makes you say that?" she hadn't even met his mother yet. There was no way she could come to that kind of a conclusion.

"Well, for one thing, the old 'do as I say, not as I do' rule." From everything she'd read about her—a great deal in the last few days—Kayla had a feeling that Lily Moreau didn't like sharing the spotlight— or her men—with another woman. "Your mom might have led an incredibly Bohemian lifestyle, but that doesn't mean she'd like the fact that her son's excuse for being late to a function she was presiding over was that he was making love to some woman."

It was, he thought, an interesting choice of words. "Is that how you think of yourself? As 'some woman'?"

Kayla had never had a problem with self-esteem. She was comfortable with who and what she was. But that was in her world, in Shelby. This was a whole new universe, filled with competitors.

She looked at him for a long moment, trying to pretend that there wasn't a great deal riding on his reply. "Don't you?"

The answer that came to mind unsettled him. Alain wasn't ready to share it with her. And because he wasn't, he suddenly realized just how serious this was. Because if it hadn't been, he would have suavely said no, adding a few lines about how special, how unique she was. Charming her. Tossing words into the wind.

But these words had weight, had substance and meaning, and that really unnerved him.

Made him feel vulnerable for the first time in a long time.

So instead, he smiled and said, "Let's go get your outfit out of the car and I'll show you to the guest room."

For a second, everything stood still. What had just happened here? Kayla wondered. Had Alain retreated? Was it happening already, his rethinking the situation and wanting to create a safe amount of distance between them?

She drew in a long breath, reminding herself that nothing was transpiring that she hadn't already anticipated twice over. She did her best to sound unaffected, even as she felt the ground crumbling beneath her.

"By the way, Mick said to tell you that your car is ready."

Her words didn't register for a beat. Right now, the sports car was the furthest thing from his mind. "Oh, right, I'd almost forgotten."

Just how rich was this man that he could forget about an expensive sports car like that? She *really* didn't belong in this world, Kayla thought.

Alain opened the front door again. "I'll have to make arrangements to pick it up."

Arrangements. Not, "I'll be there next week to get it." Arrangements.

That meant he was going to send someone else to get the car. So much for seeing him back in her neck of the woods, she thought cynically.

Kayla had no doubt, as she led the way back to the truck parked by the curb, that after tonight, more than likely, she would never see Alain again.

Lily Moreau's house, like the woman herself, was awe-inspiring. Lavish, it stopped just inches shy of overstepping the boundaries and being overdone. Made to look like a home along the French Rivera, the building stood three stories high.

The driveway of Mediterranean-blue-and-gray paving stones, circled a fountain that would have easily dwarfed most structures. Here, it appeared to fit right in. The tennis court in the back shared landscaping with an Olympic-size pool she'd expressly built for guests.

Everything both inside and outside the impressive building was pristine. White was her trademark and it was everywhere. It made the blasts of color that much more dramatic when they appeared.

"Ready?"

Alain's question penetrated the haze in Kayla's brain as she tried to take everything in at once—and tell herself that the woman got dressed the same way as everyone else. Kayla realized that he had come around to her side and was holding the passenger door opened.

A valet had slipped in on the driver's side to take his rented vehicle away.

"Ready," Kayla replied, with far more conviction than she felt.

Taking her arm, Alain tucked it through his own. "Don't think of her as a celebrity," he whispered into her ear. "Just think of her as my mother."

And that, Kayla thought, was exactly the problem. The celebrity she could deal with. The mother…

He's not bringing you home to Mother, this is just a party with an excuse. It doesn't matter whether or not she likes you. A week from now, this'll all be a faint memory, nothing more.

The knot in Kayla's stomach loosened a little.

The moment she walked into the foyer, Kayla saw it was a house built around Lily Moreau's paintings. The same splashes of color on the canvases that graced the entryway and the walls beyond were reproduced in the marble floor and the furnishings.

There was beauty everywhere she looked. It was a little like heaven—with a twist.

"You look gorgeous," Alain whispered in her ear. He was repeating himself, but thought she needed the reassurance. As if dropping his jaw when he first saw her emerge from the guest room in the slinky, silver-and-blue gown that lovingly hugged every curve she had wasn't enough.

She flashed him a grateful smile and he struggled with the surge of desire that fought to take possession of him. There would be time enough for that after the gala.

It couldn't get here soon enough for him.

And then, as if on cue, he saw his family moving forward, en masse, converging all around them. "Brace yourself," he whispered.

It seemed to Kayla that half the room had suddenly descended on her. She tightened her grip on Alain's arm, even though she'd promised herself not to let this event make her feel like a fish out of water. Catching her reflection in a mirror that hung on one side, she decided the smile she forced to her lips looked genuine enough.

And then it froze.

Lily Moreau was coming her way. Though barely five foot two, in person she appeared larger than life. Wearing a flowing, winter-white silk caftan with threads of purple shot through it to highlight her eyes, the renowned artist looked like an empress descending upon her court.

Before Kayla could murmur a heartfelt "Save me" into Alain's ear, Lily had taken her hand in both of hers, trapping her not just physically, but with her eyes.

"So this is the woman who saved my son's life." She smiled, and it seemed to Kayla as if the sun was rising across a dark lake, its rays reflected in the shimmering waters.

Kayla was relieved that she hadn't begun to shift from foot to foot. "That's a little dramatic," she replied quietly.

Lily laughed. "They tell me so am I."

Alain stepped in. "Let the others meet her before you overwhelm her, Mother."

"It is not my intention to overwhelm her, Alain. I just wish to thank her." She made no effort to release Kayla's hand.

Kayla looked down at their clasped hands, then at Lily. "I'm not going to run away, I promise."

The woman laughed and, inclining her head, stepped back. Alain was quick to draw Kayla to his side. "Kayla, you've already met Philippe. This is his fiancée, Janice. And this is my brother, Georges—"

"The doctor," Kayla stated, shaking his hand.

"You've researched us," Philippe commented.

"I like knowing things," she replied with a smile.

Lily nodded. "Very commendable." Then she glanced at Alain. "You're too slow." With that, she rattled off the names of the others, sweeping over Vienna, Janice's brother, Gordon, and the assorted nephews-in-law that three husbands had netted her. "Done," she declared, turning her attention back to Kayla. "Now, let's chat." With that, she tucked Kayla's hand through her arm and led her off to a more private area of the large room.

"Don't you think you should save her?" Georges murmured.

But Alain merely watched the two women as they took over a corner. "Kayla can hold her own." He saw Philippe studying him. "What?"

"Nothing," his older brother responded, then smiled that all-knowing smile that used to get under Alain's skin when they were teenagers.

"Don't give me 'nothing,'" he retorted. "You've got that I-know-something-you-don't look on your face."

Philippe's smile only widened. "Maybe I do," he allowed, "if you don't realize that this girl is different."

"Woman," Janice interjected patiently. "We're called women."

"Yeah." Kelli chimed in, tugging on the bottom of Philippe's jacket until he looked down at her. "We're women."

"Well, 'little woman'—" he bent down to pick up the child he'd already adopted in his heart "—let's see about getting you some cake to keep that mouth of yours busy."

Kelli tucked her arm around his neck and happily nestled in. "Okay."

Philippe glanced over his shoulder at Alain just before he walked over to the table laden with desserts. "She has my approval."

"Mine, too," Georges echoed, clapping him on the back.

Alain had suddenly become the center of attention, and he wasn't all that sure he liked it. "Not that I need it, but exactly what does Kayla have your approval for?"

"Joining the family," Georges answered, since Philippe was out of earshot. He threaded his fingers through Vienna's. "I've got to say I never thought it would happen."

Alain could feel himself growing defensive. That in itself was unusual. He'd never felt the need to before. "It's not happening now. This is a fund-raiser for homeless dogs, not a meet-Alain's-future-wife party."

"Keep telling yourself that, Alain," Georges laughed.

Remy joined the conversation, draping an arm over his younger cousin's shoulders. "If I were you, I'd take a look in the mirror."

"Why?" Alain looked down at his shirtfront, assuming that he'd gotten it dirty somehow.

Remy's grin grew wider. "Well, from where I'm standing, you look like a pretty smitten guy."

"Smitten?" Alain echoed. He stopped watching Kayla and his mother and now looked from his brother to his cousin. Behind Remy, his other cousins, Beau and Vincent, were both nodding their heads. "What are you talking about?"

Vienna surprised him by joining the conversation. She affectionately pressed her hand to his cheek. "The look in your eyes," she told him. "It does say a lot."

He was fond of Vienna, the same way he was fond of Philippe's fiancée. Both of his brothers had lucked out. But *he* was not about to be talked into anything. Even if there was a slight chance that what they were all suggesting was true.

"It says that you're all imagining things."

But even as Alain said it, he had the uncomfortable feeling that he was protesting too much—and that they all knew it.

Chapter Fourteen

Despite the attempts of several women at the fund-raiser to entice Alain to leave with them, he continued to mingle, always keeping Kayla in his line of sight. In case she needed him.

From where he stood, she seemed to be doing fine, but that could just be an act. The famous were intermixed with the not-so-famous at this last-minute gathering his mother had thrown together. Many of these people had drifted in and out of his life, as they had his mother's, for as long as he could remember.

But until tonight, he had never realized how unusual seeing all these celebrities in one place might seem to someone who'd lived most of her life in a small town where the most well-known person was probably the town sheriff.

Was she overwhelmed? Starstruck? Gilbert Holland was very hot on the Hollywood scene, and right now, the handsome actor was giving Kayla the benefit of his charismatic smile.

The surge of jealousy that washed over Alain surprised him. It took him several seconds to bank it down.

Craning his neck, he continued watching the trio. Gilbert was dominating the conversation, gesturing and looking particularly seductive. Alain couldn't tell if Kayla was responding. Well, responding or not, this had been going on for over an hour. It was high time that he rescued her, he decided.

Besides, he wanted Kayla to himself before Gilbert or someone else decided to sweep her off her feet.

Shouldering past several people who called out to him, Alain made his way to where Kayla and his mother were standing. Gilbert, he noted, looked mildly curious as he glanced up.

An image of two male bucks locking horns flashed through Alain's mind. Reaching Kayla, he placed his hand on her shoulder, his message clear as he nodded a greeting to the actor.

Gilbert took his cue and withdrew, but not before saying, "Add my pledge to the tally, Lily. Wonderful meeting you, Kayla."

Alain kept his hand where it was, drawing Kayla closer to him. "All right, Mother. Let her up for air." His tone was mild, but he wasn't about to take no for an answer.

Lily had spent the last hour-plus steering her son's young woman from one circle of friends to another, becoming increasingly more taken with Kayla as she listened to her speak. She liked the streak of steely determination she detected just beneath the surface. Alain was the most like her, and he would need a strong hand to keep him close to home.

"Air?" she echoed, looking at the young woman who was so artfully championing these dogs she and her associates rescued. "She's breathing just fine. And we're networking, aren't we, Kayla?"

Part of Kayla felt as if she was dreaming. This *had* to be the way Cinderella had felt walking into the ballroom filled with elegantly dressed people who belonged to a world she could only fantasize about. The house was littered with individuals she had read about in the pages of *People* magazine. And Alain's mother was introducing her around as if she were one of them. Very heady stuff. It took some effort to remember why she was here.

In response to Lily's comment about networking, she grinned as she looked at Alain and said, "Yes, we are."

His mother, Alain noticed, seemed exceedingly

pleased with herself. But there was something more going on, something he couldn't quite get hold of yet. He continued studying her.

"Tell him how much we've gotten in pledges so far," Lily urged.

Numbers had been flying at her right and left. The generosity overwhelmed her even more than the people did. "I lost count at fifty thousand," Kayla confessed.

"I didn't," Lily announced. Born to poverty, she was ever conscious of money. The fact that she was given to spending it lavishly when the mood hit her didn't alter that. Despite having an accountant, she kept her own tallies. "Sixty-two thousand, seven hundred. So far," she added smugly. It was obvious she thought they would do much better by evening's end. Her next words confirmed it. Leaning her head toward Kayla, who was several inches taller, she said, "The night is still young."

"Only if you're in Hawaii, Mother," Alain patiently pointed out. It was past eleven, and despite her beaming smile, Kayla looked a little worn around the edges. "I'd still like to claim her."

Lily sighed and gestured for him to take the young woman from her side. "If you must. If we played tug-of-war with this lovely creature, tongues would wage and words would somehow leak to those horrid tabloids."

Alain hadn't stopped studying his mother. The

glimmer of sadness in her eyes became apparent as she delivered her last line. Ever the dramatic grande dame, she had underlying seriousness to her tonight.

He glanced around the gathering, swiftly scanning the guests. Ordinarily, he wouldn't have to look more than a few feet to find who he was searching for.

"Where's Kyle?"

Lily took a breath, as if to launch into a long tale, then apparently changed her mind. "Not here," she said simply.

"I can see that." Alain lowered his voice so that only his mother and Kayla could hear him. "Why?" The young, so-called artist had been his mother's shadow ever since he had come into her life. He wouldn't have missed a gathering like this. "This is his element."

Lily made a disparaging sound under her breath. "I found Kyle 'in his element' earlier today." She saw Alain raise an eyebrow, urging her to elaborate. To buffer the pain, she clung to her anger, using it like a shield. "That little groupie who's been coming to the gallery every day to admire his work. She decided to 'admire' it a little closer today." Lily's carefully made-up lips twisted in disgust. "When I came by to surprise him, I was the one surprised." And then a strange smile curved her mouth, devoid of humor, tinged with triumph. "Although, I must say, it was probably a toss-up as to who was more surprised.

His groupie lost the ability to speak. So did some of the people in the immediate vicinity of the gallery." Alain was about to ask why when she told him. "Usually you have to go to Venice Beach to see a naked man running down the street." Her tone changed, as if she was talking about someone who was merely an acquaintance and not the man she had taken into her heart.

"The last I saw of Kyle, he was trying to make a policeman understand how he came to be separated from his pants." She raised her chin, a queen sharing a not-so-amusing anecdote with her court. "I hope, for his sake, he was more forthcoming with the officer than he tried to be with me."

As much as he and his brothers held Kyle suspect, Alain felt bad about the situation. Not for Kyle, but for his mother. He *hated* seeing her hurt. Even though she would never say as much, he could feel it.

Turning his back to block the view of other people in the room, he put his hand on her arm. "Are you all right?"

Lily tossed her head, her famous black mane flying over her shoulder. "I am wonderful," she declared. "I have just lost a hundred and seventy-two pounds of unnecessary weight and—" her eyes shifted to Kayla "—I have a cause to sponsor."

Out of the blue, Kayla suddenly asked, "Would you like a dog?"

The question took Lily by surprise. "Darling, you don't have to try to sell me—"

"No, I'm serious," she interrupted. "There is nothing like the unconditional love you get from a pet." Because she had been so wonderful to her tonight, Kayla decided to share something very personal with this dynamic woman. "I don't know what I would have done without mine when I had my breakup."

Alain's ears perked up at this mention of a man in her past. He had no idea why he'd imagined himself the first to have discovered her, but he had. "Break-up?"

Kayla had an uneasy feeling that she was suddenly walking on a tightrope and working without a net. But she needed to say this to Lily. "I was really shaken up, stunned that I could have misjudged someone so much."

Lily laughed shortly. "There is a lot of that going around."

Kayla deliberately avoided looking at Alain. "The man I thought I was going to spend forever with didn't turn out to be anything like I thought he was."

Lily rolled her eyes heavenward. "Amen," she murmured.

"I already had a dog to comfort me, but then someone from the rescue society asked me if I'd be willing to take in a couple of German shepherds until permanent homes could be found for them. They thought that being a vet, I wouldn't mind doing it for a few weeks. Well, my dog would lick my tears off my face, but Lenny and Squiggy wouldn't let me feel sorry for myself. And they were so tremendously grateful for any attention, any affection I showed them. I think we all kind of healed each other."

"Lenny and Squiggy?" Alain echoed. He couldn't contain the laughter that followed. Why would she have called the dogs after two hapless characters from an old classic sitcom?

"I didn't name them," Kayla protested. "The society likes to give them new names to signify their new life. But they just about saved mine." And then she got down to the heart of the matter. The people at the fund-raiser were generously giving money, but she needed homes for the dogs as much as she needed donations. "I have a lovely purebred who's eighteen months old and needs a loving home. She was abused by her owner. He all but starved her to death. Audrey is yours for the asking. I promise you, she can fill up a lot of space inside you, until you don't feel empty anymore."

Lily was silent for a long moment, and Kayla became uneasy that she might have crossed the line with her enthusiasm. "I come on strong sometimes," she began to apologize, but got no further.

"And that, my dear, is a very good trait," Lily declared in no uncertain terms. "Don't let anyone tell you otherwise. You have to push in this world to get anywhere." It was obvious that she was thinking of her own journey, as well. "All right," she said with feeling, "I'll take this—Audrey, did you say?" Kayla nodded. "I'll take Audrey in—as long as you let me pay for her," she qualified.

"There's no fee," Kayla protested. Especially not after the amount of money Lily had raised for her.

The woman didn't seem to hear. "I can write you a check for five thousand dollars. Will that be satisfactory?"

Kayla opened her mouth to protest, but Alain interrupted. "That'll be fine, Mother," he assured her as he began to steer Kayla away. "Just make it out to the German Shepherd Rescue Society, like all the other donations tonight."

His arm around Kayla's waist, Alain ushered her toward the buffet table. As he forged a path through the wall of people, he deliberately swung past Philippe and Janice. He scarcely broke stride as he told his brother, "Kyle's been eighty-sixed. Go talk to Mother, tell her something to make her feel good, the way you always do."

Philippe, holding a sleeping Kelli in his arms, turned around, surprised. "What happened?"

"From what she said, this Kyle person cheated on

her," Kayla said, before Alain had a chance to. Her heart went out to Alain's mother. She hated seeing anyone in pain.

"Oh, your poor mom." Putting down her glass of punch, Janice turned on her heel and began to make her way toward Lily. Philippe fell into step behind his fiancée.

Kayla watched the duo until they reached Lily. "How long were your mother and Kyle together?"

Alain thought for a second, working his way backward. "About six, seven months. She was with him longer than a lot of the others." He tried to sound casual about it, knowing that a lot of people judged his mother and saw her actions in a less than flattering light. But there was no way to sugar-coat it. "Mother goes through men like someone with a head cold goes through a box of tissues. But we all thought—worried—that this one was serious. I know that he thought he was." Alain would have been willing to bet on it. He'd seen it so many times before, especially in the cases he handled. An older person, trying to hang on to youth, ultimately being taken advantage of by a younger con artist.

The case he was working on now fit the bill, he thought abruptly.

"So did she," Kayla said, looking toward the artist. Philippe and Janice had just joined her.

"Listen, I'm a stranger to her, but if you want to go and be with her, I'll understand."

Alain shook his head. Philippe was better at that sort of thing than he was. "I think that pet you offered to give her will do more good than I could. Besides, this has an upside to it—other than not having to call a money-hungry SOB 'daddy,'" he qualified. "My mother will probably paint something utterly magnificent and move on."

Kayla had read that some of the world's greatest artists did their best work while in the depths of distress. "Is that how she usually handles her heartache?"

He nodded. One of her most famous paintings had been created right after she'd heard that Georges's father had died. That was when he'd realized that she never quite stopped loving any of the men who'd been in her life. "Pretty much."

"Maybe I should give her Audrey after she finishes the painting." A smile played on Kayla's lips. "We don't want to deprive the art community."

He knew she was kidding. But the concern he saw in her eyes about a woman she hardly knew, touched him. The bantering words faded from his lips.

"You're a really nice person," he told her softly, "you know that?"

"Yes, that much I know."

The way she said it, it sounded like something she

had taken to heart after having gone through a learning experience. "About that breakup you mentioned—"

She waved a hand, as if to dismiss it. "Happened a long time ago."

Ordinarily, he didn't pry. He believed in privacy, his own most importantly. Besides, not knowing made things less personal. But he didn't want to be less personal, not with Kayla. "How bad was it?"

Remembering was like walking on glass, barefoot. But if she was evasive, he was going to think that she was hiding things. The only thing she wanted to hide was her own stupidity.

"On a scale of one to ten?" she finally asked.

He nodded. "If that works for you, okay."

She sighed. "Twelve."

Something inside his chest sank. "You loved him that much?"

She looked at Alain sharply. Lost in her own thoughts, she hadn't realized how he might interpret her answer. "Oh, no. No," she repeated with feeling. "The twelve rating is based on how hard it was for me to get rid of him—physically. I had to move." *Flee* would have been a better word, she thought.

The facts weren't fitting together for him. "I thought you said you lived in that house forever."

"I have." She'd been born there, and now it was her haven, as well. "But there was a break in time when I went upstate to get my degree." She'd been accepted by several veterinary colleges. Fate had her deciding to attend the one she'd chosen. "I met Brett in San Francisco." She could see Alain was waiting for more. "And I lived there with him even after I graduated."

Jealousy snaked through his belly, burrowing in. "How long?"

"Long enough to learn I'd made a mistake." A rueful smile played on her lips. What would life have been like for her had she gone to school in San Diego? Or even out of state? "First seven months were very good. Perfect." And they had been. Which made the months that followed even more awful. "He was warm, funny, attentive." The rueful smile faded as she remembered, even as she tried to keep her thoughts at bay. "And then he began to relax."

Alain didn't follow her. "Relax?"

Kayla nodded. Music began to softly play in the background. In the distance, a dance floor was being cleared. But she stood there, on the edge of her past, trying not to let the memory of that period of time draw her into darkness.

"His facade. There was a temper, a rather bad one, that he'd been keeping under wraps. Once he thought he had me, he stopped trying to bank it down." She frowned. "He had a tendency to shout when he was angry, and he was angry almost all the time," she remembered.

Alain wanted to ask her why she didn't leave, but he wanted to know something else even more. "Did he hit you?"

Kayla hated this, hated remembering a time she was ashamed of. It was a side of herself she hadn't known existed, a side that was weak. Vulnerable. Dependant. After it was over, after it was behind her, she'd sworn to herself never to be weak again. Not like that. Not to the point where her self-respect was sacrificed.

Shrugging, she looked away, not wanting to see pity in Alain's eyes.

"A shove here, a slap there. Nothing to really leave marks," she added quickly, knowing that was no justification. "I told myself it was stress doing it to him, that he didn't mean it. That if I only made life easier for him, he wouldn't lose his temper, wouldn't get so angry." What an idiot she'd been. It wasn't anything that countless other women didn't think, didn't feel, but it made it no easier to live with.

Alain wanted to protect her, to gather her in his arms and make her forget it ever happened. More than that, he wanted to beat into a bloody pulp the snake who'd made her feel this way.

"What made you finally leave?"

The rueful smile was back as she raised her head and looked at him. "He hit the dog."

"Your pet?" he guessed. It made sense. She wouldn't put up with his doing something to a defenseless animal.

She nodded. "A stray I'd brought home with me. He was pathetic," she remembered fondly. "Skinny, malnourished, with sores on half his body. I knew I had to save him, to make him better. Brett almost lost it when I brought the dog home, but I managed to convince him to him stay.

"That last night I was there he really lost his temper over something. I can't remember what anymore." She shrugged. "Something stupid. It was always something stupid. Anyway, he swung, and I moved out of his way. He wound up hitting the dog. The dog whimpered, Brett yelled some more, and something just snapped inside of me. The next morning, I waited until he was at work and then I cleared out my stuff from the apartment, took Petey and never looked back."

Alain assumed Petey had to be the dog. "He didn't try to find you?"

She shook her head. "I don't think his ego would have been able to process the fact that I'd left him. And he never asked where I'd lived before, so he couldn't track me down." Nevertheless, she'd spent a very edgy twelve months before she felt remotely safe.

"How long ago was that?"

"Five years." She knew it down to the day, but

didn't bother adding on the months, weeks and days. "I got involved in the rescue society shortly after that." She smiled and the serious aura around her vanished. "And the rest is history."

"What happened to Petey?" Alain was pretty sure he hadn't heard her refer to any of the dogs in the house by that name. Had her pet died?

"I gave him to a little girl who'd just lost her mother." Kayla shrugged casually. "Seemed like the thing to do. She needed him more than I did. They're inseparable now," she added.

Moved, Alain found that words failed him. She seemed to do that to him, make his stock-in-trade disappear. So instead of talking, he leaned over and kissed her.

It was a soft, sweet kiss that nonetheless made her pulse jump in anticipation. When Alain drew back, she looked at him, stunned but pleased. "What was that for?"

He slipped his arm around her waist, a bevy of emotions all elbowing each other out of the way. "For being you."

That confused her. But it was a nice confusion, she thought. "All right."

It had been one hell of a party. By the time it was over, they'd garnered, according to Lily, close to ninety-five thousand dollars in pledges. Hailing from an area where people thought five thousand dollars was a great deal of money, the sum was staggering to Kayla.

But even more important than the money was the fact that she had also managed to place nearly thirty dogs with people on the strength of her recommendations—sight unseen.

"You're quite a saleswoman." There was admiration in Alain's voice.

Even though the words were flattering, Kayla found it really hard to concentrate.

They were back at his place, in his bed, and as he spoke, he was slowly stroking her. They'd already made love once, but she could feel herself responding to him all over again. Wanting to make love again. Never wanting to stop.

God, but it was glorious, being here with him like this.

"I'd rather think of myself as a matchmaker," she told him, doing her best to sound as if she didn't have a care in the world. "Matching up people with pets that are going to make their lives warmer, nicer." She turned toward him, smiling. "There's nothing as soothing as stroking a dog's fur."

He played his fingers along her body and grinned. "You might be onto something there," he agreed. "Because I don't feel soothed right now." He propped himself up on his elbow. "I feel exceedingly aroused."

"So what are we going to do about that?"

"Guess."

She didn't have to. He was already showing her.

Chapter Fifteen

Ever since he could remember, Alain had been an extremely heavy sleeper. Thunderstorms and sirens were known to leave him unaroused. When they were much younger, Philippe had commented more than once that Alain could probably sleep through the Apocalypse if it happened in their lifetime.

Which was why he hadn't woken up when Kayla left his bed.

The midmorning Sunday sun had long since pushed its way into every corner of the bedroom, warming it and him, before he finally, reluctantly, opened his eyes.

And immediately saw that the space beside him was empty.

"Kayla?"

When there was no answer, Alain raised his voice and called her name again. With the same results.

Winchester was on the floor next to his side of the bed, pressed flat on the rug as if he'd been run over by a steamroller. When Alain swung his legs down, the dog was instantly awake, instantly ready to go.

But as eager to please as the he was, the German shepherd couldn't answer the question his master shot in his direction. "Where is she, boy? Where's Kayla?"

Kayla had certainly made a believer out of him, Alain thought, mildly amused. She had him asking the dog to take him to her.

Winchester's only response was to wag his tail and present his head to be petted. Alain spared him one quick scratch behind the ears before he padded across the rug to investigate Kayla's whereabouts.

The bathroom door was wide open. He didn't have to look in to know she wasn't there, but did, anyway.

With a sigh, he grabbed a pair of jeans from the closet and pulled them on. Closing the snap, he noticed that the clothes he'd worn last night and discarded with abandonment were no longer flung every which way on the floor. Instead, they were neatly folded and piled on his bureau. Nesting instincts? He could hope so.

But then he saw that her gown, which had adhered sensuously to her body like a glimmering second skin, and which he'd more than happily peeled off, was nowhere to be seen. Had she decided to wear it again this morning, to make last night's enchantment spin out a little longer?

Something told him he was building castles in the air.

"Kayla?"

Alain checked the guest room and saw that the clothes she'd worn when she had arrived yesterday were gone, as well.

Uneasiness began to skitter through him like an insect across a checkered linoleum floor.

Was this the answer she'd promised to give him? The one in response to the proposal that had popped out of his mouth?

Somewhere in the dead of night, after the lovemaking had left him enveloped in a sweet, seductive afterglow, he'd heard himself whispering words to her he never thought he'd say to any woman.

"Will you marry me?"

The moment the question was out, he'd felt Kayla stiffen against him, as if she was expecting a physical blow. And then she'd laughed as she relaxed again. "You've had too much to drink."

He'd caressed her face, wanting to make love with her again. But he was far too exhausted to attempt it. As for the alcohol, maybe he'd had a tiny bit more than usual. He'd let her drive them home, but he was by no means too intoxicated to know what he was saying.

"Maybe that's what's giving me the courage to ask," he'd told her. And maybe, in hindsight, that had been a wee bit too honest. But he felt he could be open with her. Felt he could be himself—without consequences. She'd made him feel so differently about everything.

"So," he'd finally pressed, when she gave him no answer, "will you? Marry me," repeated, in case she'd lost sight of the question during the silence.

"I'll let you know in the morning," she'd promised, and he'd heard the smile in her voice. A smile that warmed him from the inside out. "If you still want to ask me."

"I will," he guaranteed with feeling, slipping his arms around her.

He fell asleep holding her.

And now here it was, morning. And he couldn't find her.

Was this her way of giving him his answer?

He felt upset; he felt relieved. He felt damn confused.

Maybe this was for the best, after all.

No, damn it, it wasn't. He *wanted* to marry her. For the first time in his life, he wanted to get married.

The irony of the situation was not lost on him.

Alain called her name again, a little more urgently this time, as he hurried down the stairs. Winchester bounded down beside him and, as always, made it to the landing first.

"Kayla!"

Alain's voice echoed back to him. "I think she left us, boy," he murmured dejectedly, striding to a window that faced the front of the house.

Her truck was no longer parked by the curb. Rather than face him, rather than face his proposal again, she'd left before he woke up.

He'd never been rejected before. Alain couldn't say he liked it.

Dragging a hand through his hair, he went to the kitchen to make coffee. If he was going to figure things out, figure out how he felt about this turn of events and what his next move was going to be, he needed coffee. Lots of coffee. Black, like the mood that was swiftly descending over him.

Kayla tried to go about her life as if it were business as usual. As if her painfully reconstructed world hadn't just experienced an 8.9 earthquake, knocking out all the foundations beneath it.

Alain had asked her to marry him. And scared the

hell out of her. Because he was asking her to risk everything, to risk having her heart ripped out of her chest again and used for soccer practice.

She sighed, shaking her head as she continued grooming Audrey, the dog she'd promised to Lily.

Brett had done a number on her, Kayla admitted. He'd made her leery of trusting her own judgment. Because of him, she was afraid to savor the simple joy of falling in love. Her fear of disappointment blocked out everything else.

So, when faced with Alain's proposal, she'd run. Run instead of answering him. Run back to what she knew.

And he hadn't tried to call her, hadn't come after her. Hadn't sent out carrier pigeons to try to get in contact with her.

It wasn't as if she'd just disappeared into thin air. She'd gone home. Alain knew where that was. And he hadn't followed her.

Which told her that it *had* been the alcohol talking that night when he'd proposed. Alcohol and nothing more. Certainly not his heart. And as each day faded into night without him calling or coming by, she grew more and more certain that she'd been right not to say yes, not to ask "How high?" when her heart had told her to jump.

And with each passing day, the gaping hole in her life just seemed to grow larger.

Unlike the last time, or whenever she was monumentally upset, working didn't help.

Nothing took her mind off Alain, or the pain she felt because he didn't care.

The way she did.

"What's the matter with me, Audrey?" she asked, annoyed with herself. She rubbed a towel against the wet fur. "I didn't even know him for that long." She rocked back on her heels, the towel in her hand. "How can you fall in love with someone so fast? I don't believe in love at first sight. Lust, maybe," she allowed, "but not love."

But it had been love, pure and simple, because she was fairly certain that lust didn't hurt this way. It didn't make you feel as if the sun had suddenly been extinguished, leaving you to find your way in the dark.

God, this felt terrible.

She realized she was crying again, and blinked, wiping away the stray tear that managed to reach her cheek.

"The next guy who crashes into a tree on my property I'm leaving there," she said, looking into Audrey's big brown eyes. The shepherd's response was to raise up on her hind legs and lick Kayla's face, and she laughed despite herself. "That was my first problem. I let him kiss me." And that was the beginning of her downfall, she thought. Because the man made the world fade away.

With a sigh, she frowned, thinking about what she had to do. She'd promised to bring Lily her new pet. And Philippe had asked for one of Ginger's puppies. The dogs needed a home more than she needed to hide. But how was she going to face these people and act as if everything was all right?

She pressed her lips together, thinking. Alain's family probably had no idea that there was anything out of the ordinary going on. Kayla was willing to bet he hadn't told any of them that he'd proposed. Or that he'd willingly let her go.

There was no question in her mind that she was going to keep her word. And she had to do it *now.* It was, she told herself, like pulling a thorn out of your hand. You had to do it quickly. The longer you delayed, the more frightening the proposition seemed, and the longer it was before you could begin healing.

With a sigh, she went to get the puppy she'd selected for Philippe, a mischievous, affectionate female she'd mentally dubbed Duchess.

She forced herself to focus on the dogs and on nothing else.

His pride hurt, Alain tried his best to forget about Kayla. But his best wasn't good enough. He just couldn't seem to shake off her influence. She'd made him see everything through different eyes. Even the cases he worked. It wasn't about winning anymore. It was about, God help him, doing the right thing.

Which was why he found himself paying a visit to Bobbie Jo Halliday. He was determined to appeal to her better nature. Even if he had to bribe her to do it.

And he wasn't about to back down until he'd hammered out something acceptable to his client that was still generous to the deceased's children. Despite what his firm might say to the contrary, this was only fair.

And Kayla had taught him how important it was to play fair.

Kayla first went to Lily's house and then to Philippe's, all the while hoping against hope that she might run into Alain, even though she told herself she'd be better off if she didn't.

Well, she didn't, and God knew she didn't feel better off. What she felt, damn him, was bereft.

The song on the radio annoyed her. All the songs on the radio annoyed her. Why did people have to keep singing about finding "the right one"?

With a huff, she switched it off.

She wished she'd brought another dog along. As it was, the loneliness was eating holes in her. Making her feel empty.

Kayla's hands tightened on the steering wheel.

The freeways were moving at a good, fast pace and she was making incredible time.

Time to do what? Return home and be hit between the eyes with how empty everything was there, as well? Despite the fact that the place was now packed with eight puppies and six adult dogs?

Why did everything feel so empty just because Alain wasn't in it? She'd lived all this time without the man. Why was it so hard to continue doing that now?

Taking the turn to her house, Kayla suddenly felt her heart leap into her throat. Joy, anticipation, excitement all vied for top position.

Someone was sitting on her doorstep. Someone who, from this distance, looked just like Alain.

But it couldn't be him. He was supposed to be at work. Wasn't he?

It *was* him, she realized, drawing closer. Her pulse was racing. Why was he here? Had he missed her, or—

And then her heart sank again. His car. He was probably in town to pick it up. But if that was the case, how had he gotten to her house? And where was the vehicle, anyway?

Sliding out of the front seat, she had to brace her wobbly knees. Kayla held on to the door a second before she finally slammed it shut. She never took her eyes off Alain, afraid that he might disappear if she did.

"Hi."

"Hi," he echoed, getting up. He'd been sitting there for almost an hour, waiting for her to come back, wrestling with his thoughts. Was he being an idiot waiting for her, or was this the smartest thing he'd ever done?

When he saw her get out of her car, he had his answer.

As he crossed to her, she asked, "Come about your car?"

His car. He'd completely forgotten about the vehicle that was languishing at the mechanic's shop. More proof that he was in love. Thoughts of this woman had taken center stage in his life, completely pushing everything else into the background.

But in order not to look like a complete fool, he lied. "Among other things."

Her heart leaped up again. *Stop hoping, idiot. If he cared, he would have been here way before this.* "What other things?"

And then, suddenly, he was blocking out the sun, blocking out everything as he looked into her eyes. "You. We have some unfinished business."

Be strong, damn it. You know this isn't going to work. She squared her shoulders. "No, we don't," she informed him quietly. "I told you I'd give you my answer in the morning." Kayla raised her chin. "And I did."

"When? How?"

"I left you a note."

"I never found a note." Although he hadn't been looking for a note, he'd been looking for her. Paper had never entered into it.

"Typical male," she murmured.

She was stalling, he thought. "So, will you repeat what you wrote, so I can hear it with my 'typical male' ears?"

It was going to be a lot harder to say this face-to-face, which was why she'd written it in the first place. She felt her courage flagging. "I don't remember exactly what I wrote—but for the record, I said something to the effect that I wouldn't hold you to a proposal that was given while you were drunk."

"I wasn't drunk," he insisted. "I had a pleasant buzz on."

Semantics, she thought. "Well, you were buzzing in my ear and—"

He wasn't about to get waylaid by rhetoric. He had to hear her say this. Maybe then he'd back away. But until he did, he was going to nurse this hope—just as his mother did each time she entered a new relationship, he realized. "You don't want to marry me?"

How could Kayla make him understand, when she didn't fully comprehend this herself? "It's not that I don't *want* to marry you. I can't marry you."

He was doing his best to understand, but it was like trying to read words through a layer of mud. "Are you already married?"

"No."

"Engaged?"

She looked away, her voice growing smaller, more distant. "No."

Then she was free, he thought. Anticipation moved to the front of the line. "Betrothed at birth to the prince of some tiny country?"

She laughed despite herself. "No."

Alain took hold of her shoulders, afraid she was going to bolt on him. "What, then?"

"I can't marry you because you weren't serious when you asked me."

That made no sense whatsoever, he thought. "Would you like me to write it in blood?"

"No, I just wanted you to mean it." But she'd learned that there was no such thing as forever. And she was afraid that the hurt would be too much for her.

He looked at her, his face completely serious. "I have a cousin who works for the FBI. He could score a lie detector machine for me for about an hour. You could hook me up."

"I—"

He took her hand in his, knowing he had to show her what was in his heart if he was ever going to win her over. He was going to have to be vulnerable in order to be strong. It made no sense to him, but he knew it was true.

"Look, I admit that I'm scared. I probably look like a deer caught in the headlights—"

She followed the unflattering metaphor to its conclusion. "And I'm the truck about to run you down?"

"Don't interrupt," he chided. "You get to make your closing argument later."

With a laugh, she shook her head. "Ever the lawyer."

"Shh." He got back to his main point. "I'm scared because I never made a commitment before. You know what I'm *more* scared of?"

"Oh, you're asking a question." A smile played on her lips. "Do I get to answer?"

He went on, never more serious in his life. "I'm more scared of living without you. I tried it and I don't like it. You've made an impression on my life, Kayla. You've placed your imprint everywhere, and nothing is the same anymore. I want you in my life. I want you right there in the morning when I wake up."

She was a realist when she had to be. And she knew she had no choice right now. Her roots were here. His were not. "And you're willing to give up your work, everything you know, to be with me? Because I can't leave here, Alain. Everyone's dependent on me. We're a small community and everyone is necessary here."

She couldn't read the look in his eyes. "Did I say

you could talk yet?" he asked her. When Kayla shook her head, he continued. "I'm not going to give up everything."

Which meant that he wanted her to pick up everything and relocate in his world. She couldn't. As lovely as it was, she couldn't. "Well, then—"

"Still no talking," he reminded her. "The firm has a helicopter. I've made inquiries, and because I just put them on the map with this settlement dealing with Ethan Halliday's will—I'll tell you about that later—they're willing to let me use the copter to fly up here at night and back to the firm's landing pad every morning. That way I won't be stuck in two hours of traffic each way, and you get to stay here."

A helicopter. "You can fly a helicopter?"

"Yes."

She was impressed. "You have an argument for everything."

For the first time since he'd begun pleading his case, Alain grinned. "I'm a lawyer, I have to. And this is the most important argument of my career." He took her into his arms. "I'm in love with you, Kayla, and I can truly say I've never been in love before. So, what about it?"

The corners of her mouth curved. "I get to talk now?"

Alain nodded. "You get to talk now—but only if you say the right thing."

She batted her eyes at him innocently. "Which would be?"

"'Yes,'" he told her.

"Then it's yes, since you're not accepting any other answers. Now let's go pick up your car."

But he wasn't about to release her just yet. There was all this unbridled desire ricocheting in his chest. Just before he lowered his mouth to hers, he assured her, "The car can wait."

And it did.

* * * * *

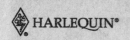

Get ready to meet

THREE WISE WOMEN

with stories by

DONNA BIRDSELL,
LISA CHILDS

and

SUSAN CROSBY.

Don't miss these three unforgettable stories about modern-day women and the love and new lives they find on Christmas.

Look for *Three Wise Women*
Available December wherever you buy books.

The Next Novel.com

REQUEST YOUR FREE BOOKS!
2 FREE NOVELS PLUS 2 FREE GIFTS!

SPECIAL EDITION®
Life, Love and Family!

YES! Please send me 2 FREE Silhouette Special Edition® novels and my 2 FREE gifts. After receiving them, if I don't wish to receive any more books, I can return the shipping statement marked "cancel." If I don't cancel, I will receive 6 brand-new novels every month and be billed just $4.24 per book in the U.S., or $4.99 per book in Canada, plus 25¢ shipping and handling per book and applicable taxes, if any*. That's a savings of at least 15% off the cover price! I understand that accepting the 2 free books and gifts places me under no obligation to buy anything. I can always return a shipment and cancel at any time. Even if I never buy another book from Silhouette, the two free books and gifts are mine to keep forever.   235 SDN EEYU 335 SDN EEY6

Name	(PLEASE PRINT)

Address	Apt.

City	State/Prov.	Zip/Postal Code

Signature (if under 18, a parent or guardian must sign)

Mail to the **Silhouette Reader Service™**:
IN U.S.A.: P.O. Box 1867, Buffalo, NY 14240-1867
IN CANADA: P.O. Box 609, Fort Erie, Ontario L2A 5X3

Not valid to current Silhouette Special Edition subscribers.

Want to try two free books from another line?
Call 1-800-873-8635 or visit www.morefreebooks.com.

* Terms and prices subject to change without notice. NY residents add applicable sales tax. Canadian residents will be charged applicable provincial taxes and GST. This offer is limited to one order per household. All orders subject to approval. Credit or debit balances in a customer's account(s) may be offset by any other outstanding balance owed by or to the customer. Please allow 4 to 6 weeks for delivery.

Your Privacy: Silhouette is committed to protecting your privacy. Our Privacy Policy is available online at www.eHarlequin.com or upon request from the Reader Service. From time to time we make our lists of customers available to reputable firms who may have a product or service of interest to you. If you would prefer we not share your name and address, please check here. ☐

Inside ROMANCE

Stay up-to-date on all your romance reading news!

Inside Romance is a FREE quarterly newsletter highlighting our upcoming series releases and promotions.

Visit
www.eHarlequin.com/InsideRomance
to sign up to receive our complimentary newsletter today!

IRN1107

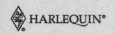

COMING NEXT MONTH

SPECIAL EDITION

#1867 THE McKETTRICK WAY—Linda Lael Miller
Meg McKettrick longed for a baby—husband optional—and her rugged old flame, rodeo cowboy Brad O'Ballivan, was perfect father material. But Brad didn't want a single night of passion, he wanted love, marriage, the works. Now it was an epic battle of wills, as proud, stubborn Meg insisted on doing things her way…the McKettrick way.

#1868 A BRAVO CHRISTMAS REUNION—Christine Rimmer
Bravo Family Ties
Try as he might, coffeehouse-chain tycoon Marcus Reid couldn't get over his former executive assistant Hayley Bravo. But when Hayley had proposed to him seven months ago, he'd balked and she'd left town. Now a business trip reunited them…and clued Marcus in to the real reason for Hayley's proposal—he was about to be a daddy!

#1869 A COWBOY UNDER HER TREE—Allison Leigh
Montana Mavericks: Striking It Rich
Hotel heiress Melanie McFarlane took over Thunder Canyon Ranch to prove she could run a successful business on her own. But she needed help—bad—and enlisted local rancher Russ Chilton, telling her family he was her husband. Russ insisted on a legal marriage to seal the deal, and soon city slicker Melanie fell hard…for her husband.

#1870 THE MILLIONAIRE AND THE GLASS SLIPPER—Christine Flynn
The Hunt for Cinderella
When his tech mogul father delivered the ultimatum to marry and have kids within a year or be disinherited, family rebel J. T. Hunt decided to set up his own business before he was cut off. For help, he turned to a bubbly blond ad exec—but it was her subtly beautiful stepsister, Amy Kelton, who rode to the rescue as J.T.'s very own Cinderella.

#1871 HER CHRISTMAS SURPRISE—Kristin Hardy
Kelly Stafford thought she was engaged to the *good* Alexander sibling—until she walked in on him with another woman, and his money laundering threatened to land Kelly in jail! Now could his black-sheep brother, Lex Alexander—voted Most Likely To Get Arrested back in high school—save Kelly…and maybe even steal her heart in the process?

#1872 THE TYCOON MEETS HIS MATCH—Barbara Benedict
Sure it was surprising when writer Trae Andrelini's independent friend Lucy decided to marry stuffed-shirted mogul Rhys Paxton for security, and even more surprising when Lucy left him at the altar to go after an old boyfriend. But the biggest surprise of all? When free-spirited Trae discovered that Rhys was actually the man for *her!*

SSECNM1107